© Jocelyn Kaye

JORDAN KAYE is a writer and lawyer with a life passion for moderate boozing. He lives with his wife, Jocelyn; their two children, Ellis and Gideon; and a sprawling collection of bottles and barware in Brooklyn, New York.

© Amy Leipziger

MARSHALL ALTIER is a bartender, a consultant, and a writer based in New York City and Hong Kong. He has been part of the opening teams of several well-known New York bars and his original creations have been featured in print in the *New York Post*'s *Page Six Magazine*, the *San Francisco Chronicle*, and *New York* magazine. He has also designed drink menus and food pairings for a variety of establishments and brands across the world.

Illustrator SAM OWENS grew up in the West Woods of the United States and now lives in Brooklyn, New York. His work can be seen at www.samowens.com

HOW TO

BOOZE

EXQUISITE COCKTAILS

AND

UNSOUND
ADVICE

HOW TO
BOOZE

JORDAN KAYE
&
MARSHALL ALTIER

With Illustrations by Sam Owens

HARPER

NEW YORK • LONDON • TORONTO • SYDNEY

HARPER

HarperCollins books may be purchased for educational, business, or sales promotional use. For information please write: Special Markets Department, HarperCollins Publishers, 10 East 53rd Street, New York, NY 10022.

FIRST EDITION

Designed by Sunil Manchikanti

Library of Congress Cataloging-in-Publication Data

Kaye, Jordan.
How to booze / Jordan Kaye & Marshall Altier. —1st Harper paperbacks ed.
    p. cm.
Includes bibliographical references and index.
ISBN 978-0-06-196330-8
1. Drinking of alcoholic beverages—Humor. I. Altier, Marshall. II. Title.

PN6231.D7K39 2010
818'.607—dc22

2009054295

10 11 12 13 14 OV/RRD 10 9 8 7 6 5 4 3 2 1

To all the lovely people
who have driven us to drink

Contents

WHY
WE BOOZE,
AND
WHY
IT MATTERS

It is a Friday evening. An old friend has just arrived for a weeklong visit, a massive wheeled suitcase in tow. Problem: it's not clear you have anything to say to each other. You are now standing in front of your unevenly populated liquor cabinet, pondering what to pour to re-grease the wheels of friendship. Your friend is waiting on the couch in the other room, possibly in a similar state of unease.

OR

Your date is pronouncing, imperiously: "I am known to be an impeccable judge of character." This date turns out to be so laughably unbearable that it might just make sense to stand up, scream with a thick accent, "I have the runs!" and goose-step out of the room with your hands cupped over your behind. But you don't do that. You bear down. You smile. And you order a drink.

OR

You have returned from your honeymoon. After all the gifts are unwrapped and you resume something like a normal routine, the relief of having the wedding behind you is accompanied by the realization that your youth has an expiration date. Somehow, suddenly, surprisingly, that's okay with you. With the recklessly expensive festivities and travel now behind you, it's time for a quieter moment of celebration, to toast to what's to come and what you are leaving behind.

OR

You are leaning over a bar, desperate for the bartender's attention. He isn't looking at you. He seems to be making some kind of sick sport out of not looking at you. He seems to be getting a euphoric high from the humiliation he is able to inflict from the simple exercise of ignoring your presence. What are the corners of his lips doing? Is he actually suppressing a smile? When he feels the farce has run its course, he finally, with great reluctance, turns to you for an order. Your moment has arrived: a chance for redemption. But even still, he looks as if he might lose interest at any time. So what do you do? You stare back blankly, feasting on the attention. And utterly paralyzed. What was it you wanted? You realize you have absolutely no idea, you *never* had any idea. The elements—rum, Scotch whisky, Irish whiskey, gin, tequila, bitters of every kind, apple brandy, sweet vermouth, dry vermouth, egg whites, lemon peels, egg yolks, orange liqueur, absinthe, vodka, twists of orange and lime—float and swirl in your mind's eye without rhyme or reason. They all have a place and a relationship and a purpose. But what's the right combination for right now? Without a clue as to the answer, you fall back on ordering your "usual," regardless of whether or not you are in the mood for it. Anything to move on with the night.

Your standoff with the bartender is thankfully resolved. But left unresolved is the feeling that there must be a specific answer: *just* the right cocktail for *just* this moment.

This book is dedicated to giving you that answer. In fact, this book is dedicated to giving you around a *hundred* answers: a whole slew of cocktails for a whole slew of situations.

But before we figure out what to drink, let's talk about *why* you drink. Alcohol presents a nearly unbeatable combination of downsides: it comes with the pronounced risk of liver disease; it is intensely caloric, highly addictive, and likely to cause unprotected sex with strangers who will almost surely bless you with incurable diseases or stupid, ugly children. All that sounds promising enough, but isn't there more?

Drinks make stories more interesting. They make families more bearable. Music sounds better, food tastes tastier, and the people around you become more attractive.

But it isn't actually the world around you that changes; it's *you* that changes. And it's not just your judgment that improves—though it unquestionably does. (The experts are wrong here.) A good drink, when it's put together right and is suited to the occasion, transforms you into a better version of yourself. The first sip is cool to the lips, perfectly balanced on the palette, and makes your blood hum as it washes down. Your brain springs unwind. You nestle into your nestling place, and you allow yourself the silent acknowledgment that some things are still okay in the world. *Still okay.*

That's what the right drink has to offer. Meanwhile, dangers abide. They lurk, waiting for you to order the wrong drink at the wrong time. Things can go bad. Bad like waking up in a Mexican jailhouse to the sound of your traveling companion screaming out in pain from an adjacent cell. Bad like a date that begins with a yawn, two rounds of beer, and a bottle of wine, and regrettably ends in your apartment with you dozing off while your new acquaintance is heading, well, south. Bad like breaking into tears of religious rapture at the office holiday party. Bad like hitting-on-your-cousin-at-your-grandmother's-wake bad.

If any of this sounds familiar, you have already gotten your first lesson in the science of booze, which is to say you have figured out that a drink that goes down perfectly in certain situations can lead to disastrous results in others. The constellation of drinks is boundless and, like the greeting card aisle at the pharmacy, provides options for every situation imaginable. Some are sickly sweet, others just plain off, and a rare few are just right.

What we are concerned about is the kind of error that might lead to ordering a Bloody Mary at a nightclub: spicy tomato juice and steak sauce are great for mornings, bad for getting your groove on. Or a grasshopper at a pub with old friends. Sweet, creamy, and minty, it's arguably never entirely respectable, but it's downright disgraceful here. And we have yet to see a shot-fueled first date that didn't end in crash-and-burn, or a Valentine's Day ski retreat successfully consummated with frozen margaritas. If any of the above works for you, then God bless. But to us, the perfect drink is worth fighting for.

Developing a feel for the perfect drink means understanding the anatomy of a cocktail—and then also the anatomy of the situation. There are times when you want to be relaxed but alert, times when you want to be wild and carefree, and other, darker times when you crave introspection. There are moments of duplicity and moments of solidarity. Meanwhile, there are drinks you just don't order from the surfer guy pulling beers at the beach. So there is plenty to explain about spirits, modifiers, lemon peels, egg whites, stirring, and shaking, but also much to say about second dates, barbecues, breakups, meeting the in-laws, and the day you get laid off from your job—all those moments that just wouldn't be the same without a stiff drink.

As an author team, we bring years of hard-earned knowledge. We've made the wrong drinks at the wrong time, the right drinks at the wrong time, gotten sick off our own concoctions, and irreversibly tarnished relationships. Trains have been missed, flights forgotten about, lawns mauled, and mailboxes crushed. Friends have been turned to lifelong foes. But we've also mixed some pretty good cocktails in our day—cocktails that have won awards, made parties rage, and brought smiles to the faces of loved ones.

We believe it's important that you use this wisdom to do more than simply remember which cocktails go with which situation—a framework that in any case is closer to a mnemonic than a code. Our aim is for something even better: we want you to have the tools to make your *own* judgments about what to drink. Even invent your own cocktails, based on whatever you have at hand and whatever you happen to be feeling at the moment.

Is cocktailing an art, or just a self-destructive pastime? Let the critics and doctors duke it out: really, it's not for us to say. But if any self-destructive pastime can be elevated to an art form, we believe we have stumbled upon it. And by picking up this book, you've stumbled upon it, too.

SPIRITS

There are two basic steps to making a spirit. First, you need to ferment something: that is, allow yeast to infect some sugary liquid and excrete alcohol (this is how wine and beer are made). Next, you distill a fermented liquid by heating it up and capturing the vapors of the alcohol that steam up first, leaving the rest behind. Condensing those vapors will yield a liquid with a higher concentration of alcohol. Distilling that concentrated liquid multiple times will yield a purer, stronger alcohol. Some combination of aging, diluting, flavoring, and filtering the resulting liquid is what makes it palatable.

fig. 1

fig. 2

fig. 3

fig. 4

fig. 5   fig. 6   fig. 7

fig. 8

GLASSWARE FOR SERVING COCKTAILS & MIXED DRINKS

fig.1—cocktail (martini); fig. 2—old-fashioned;
fig. 3—highball; fig. 4—Collins; fig. 5—flute;
fig. 6—cordial; fig. 7—cocktail (coupe); fig. 8—wine

When cocktails first came into vogue, they were typically served in a coupe. The so-called martini-style glass became popular in the mid-twentieth century. We prefer the coupe for the practical reason that it's less prone to spill. The coupe's gentle curves also show off a dink's color and shine.

THE
BASIC
SKILLS

We will introduce skills and factoids as the need arises. But there are a few things you really must know before we get going.

CHILLING GLASSWARE

Chilling your glassware is the essential first step in preparing any drink that is served without ice. It ensures a cold sip, makes you look like you know what you're doing, and gives you time to ponder what the hell you're going to make. Simply fill the glass with four ice cubes and a splash of cold water before you start mixing. When you are ready to pour your drink, dump the ice and give the glass a good sharp flick over the sink to ensure that a minimum of moisture is left in the glass.

If you have freezer space to spare, you can also freeze your glasses. Rather surprisingly, just three or four minutes in the freezer will give a glass a good frost. And you will definitely land with a very chilly drink, if not a pile of glass shards in your freezer.

Cocktail glasses should always be chilled, but don't forget to chill champagne flutes, too—particularly important when you are mixing a champagne cocktail that calls for 2 or 3 ounces of room temperature spirit to be poured directly into the glass. For drinks that are served in a highball or old-fashioned glass *over fresh ice* (and not all are, see **Sazerac**), chilling is less important but may still feel like the right thing to do on a hot day.

MEASURING

A small, clear measuring cup—the kind typically used for cooking or baking—is more useful than a jigger.

SIMPLE SYRUP

Simple syrup is used in many recipes as a sweetening agent. The recipe goes like this: one part fine sugar to one part hot water. Stir.

Make plenty for yourself: a bottle will keep refrigerated for at least a month or, if spiked with a small dash of neutral grain alcohol (e.g., unflavored vodka), far longer. For recipes that call for a "rich" simple syrup, add another bit of sugar.

If you are terribly lazy and degenerate, you can always just use a spoonful of sugar instead of simple syrup. But we must protest: the sweetness mixes far more evenly into an iced cocktail when the sugar is already diluted into syrup. That being said, we will point out some recipes that specifically call for sugar.

If you are only moderately lazy and degenerate, and can't be bothered making simple syrup ahead of time but would like to put in your best effort when the need arises, remember this: a lot of recipes call for ¾ ounce of simple syrup. There are about two measured tablespoons to an ounce. So for these recipes, you will want to mix about ¾ tablespoon (or roughly 3 teaspoons)—*each* of sugar and warm water. This isn't totally precise, but it's close enough for a lazy boozer like you.

JUICING

A variety of contraptions can be used for squeezing the bejesus out of a lemon or lime. Whatever you use, for nearly all recipes you will want your juice thoroughly strained, since pulp can really drag down the quality of the drink. Most squeezers do only a fair to middling job of straining. Since this part is really important, use a very fine wire cooking strainer to remove the pulp before pouring the juice into the mixing glass.

MIXING

The best tool for mixing is a classic Boston shaker: one large glass and one slightly larger tin. Some glasses have measuring lines, which allows you to avoid messing up a separate measuring cup or jigger. If you are holed up in a cabin twisted up on methamphetamines or otherwise short of tools, a clean glass jar with a screw top will work just fine.

Not to torture you with the obvious, but when we say "shake" or "stir," we mean to do so with ice. So build the drink in the mixing glass without ice (this allows you to measure as you pour, especially if your mixing glass has measuring lines) and then add *plenty* of ice—don't be stingy.

While you are always free to experiment, there is usually a good reason why a drink should be stirred rather than shaken or vice versa: it really *does* make a difference. Stirring allows delicate, carefully balanced flavors to shine; shaking brings in a lot of oxygen and sparkle and slivers of ice. The general rule of thumb is that if the mixed ingredients are clear, stir; if cloudy (usually because of the addition of citrus juice), shake.

To **shake**, clamp down the tin on top of the glass and set to work for about fifteen to twenty seconds. And give yourself a real workout. As famed Prohibition-era cocktail master Harry Craddock wrote in *The Savoy Cocktail Book*, "Shake the shaker as hard as you can; don't just rock it; you are trying to wake it up, not send it to sleep!" A seal forms between the glass and tin, so separating the two pieces can take some work. At this point make sure the tin is on the bottom and the glass is on the top: this way, since the tin is larger than the glass, you won't have any spillage when they detach. Now hold the shaker set in your nondominant hand, cradling your index and middle fingers around the back for support. Then give the tin's edge a few good whacks with the heel of your dominant hand.

Stirring takes longer, since the ice won't melt as fast. So commit to it for at least twenty-five to thirty seconds. A long, thin bar spoon is the best instrument, but of course just use what you have.

GARNISHING WITH LEMON PEEL

Though the amount of oil it releases is minuscule, a lemon peel adds a central flavor component. If you are going for a visually perfect peel, the process is unfortunately going to piss you off. Two kinds of peels are possible: one long, thin peel, which you will twist over your drink to release its oils before placing it into the glass (you can also wrap it around a swizzle stick, to coil it); or a shorter, wide peel (or a "boat," since that's what it should resemble), which you will lightly fold over the drink and then press along the glass's rim. Our preference is for the boat—for mostly superficial reasons, though it also happens to be the easier technique. Generally you want as little of the bitter white lining, or pith, as possible—but getting neurotic about it is sure to leave you frustrated and, if you are on your second or third drink, bloodied.

The good news is that the most important part of the peel is the oil it releases. So even if your peels more closely resemble the ungraceful chunks of skin now littering your kitchen floor, your peel will still be a success as long as you are able to squeeze it, outside skin pointing directly onto the surface of the drink, so that the oils spray drinkward. Blood optional.

Instructions

For a long, thin peel, use your thumb to guide a sharp knife around the circumference of the citrus—keep your eye close on the blade for greater control. For a boat, peel from the top of the fruit to the bottom. A wider knife will allow you to take off a wider, longer piece; a narrower knife will allow more control in avoiding pith. A boat can also be prepared with a vegetable peeler—this is probably the easiest way, and it is common even among professional bartenders.

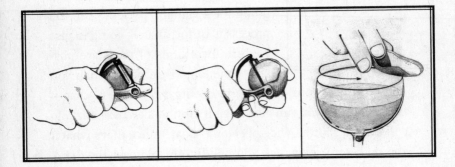

Stage 1

Love
Needs
Drink

FIRST DATE

Ships that pass in the night, and speak each other in passing;
Only a signal shown and a distant voice in the darkness;
So on the ocean of life, we pass and speak one another,
Only a look and a voice, then darkness again and a silence.

Henry Longfellow said that. But he was paid by the word, so he tended to ramble. Translation: "First dates are bullshit."

It turns out Longfellow wasn't just an expert on virginal natives. He knew something about dating, too. Because first dates are pretty much like ships passing in the night: strangers before, an hour or two of *blah-blah-blah*, an awkward cheek-kiss-half-hug thing, then a warmly worded text message. And then silence. Strangers before, strangers after.

But there are differences between passing ships and first dates. One difference is that, on a date, there is at least a sporting chance of sex; the only hope of sex for passing ship passengers is if there's a collision, both boats sink, two very hard-up survivors wind up on the same lifeboat, and everyone else on the lifeboat is hypothermic. This was the ending to *Titanic* everyone was hoping for.

The other difference between passing ships and first dates is that first dates involve alcohol—and it's a good thing they do. The right drink—slow sipping, calming on the nerves but heady enough to liven things up—can create just the sort of false intimacy everyone craves.

Dark 'n' Stormy

2 OZ GOSLING'S BLACK SEAL BERMUDA RUM (6 CL)
GINGER BEER

Build in highball glass filled with ice. Top up with ginger beer.

Garnish with wedge of lime.

Remember, there is a reason you are paying a hefty monthly fee to belong to an online dating service. Yes, it's fun to sit at a computer and objectify strangers for hours at a time. But you stay with it—and keep going on all those first dates—on that off chance that false intimacy might, over time, lead to *real* intimacy. To honor that enduring hope, we give you the Dark 'n' Stormy.

The "official drink" of Bermuda (we have a weakness for countries with official drinks), the Dark 'n' Stormy is fun and easy to sip—in fact, a more appropriate name would be "Light and Breezy." With just two ingredients, no pretense, and the adventuresome warm spice of ginger to keep things interesting, this is a great companion drink for getting to know someone.

Gosling's is a dark rum made in the English style, popular in former outposts of the British empire like Bermuda. The only catch with the Dark 'n' Stormy is that ginger beer can be hard to find. Reed's, produced in Jamaica, is a widely available option; Gosling's now creates its own drier and spicier brew.

If you find yourself eager to show your wild side this early on, you can modify the Dark 'n' Stormy by adding an extra dose of lime juice. Juice the lime with a hand press. This will give you a spent half shell that, once turned inside out, can be placed on top of the drink with an extra "float" of rum inside for the brave-hearted.

RUM, TEQUILA, AND "WHAT THE HELL HAVE I DONE?" BLACKOUTS

Rum and tequila are distinct from other spirits in that they cover a broader range. Some are totally colorless ("white" or "silver"), because they are aged for a minimal amount of time (if at all) and then, in the case of rum, filtered. Others run from amber to dark because they are aged for longer periods of time—but the truth is that some are dyed with caramel to make you feel tougher and fancier when you drink them. Most cocktail recipes that call for rum or tequila will flourish differently depending on how dark your base spirit is, so feel free to experiment.

So why do tequila and rum lead to so many wild nights and heinously poor choices? Honestly, we only wish we knew.

YOU WILL REGRET THIS; YOU *ALREADY* REGRET THIS

It can be grim work, bedding down the homely. But the truly unattractive *do* have the right to sex. And sometimes, it's just your turn to give it to them. Others shirk their duty; you are worthier than that. Where lesser folk yawn and slip out the door, you buy two more rounds and bravely step up to the challenge.

Verbal overtures are cast and received. Trembling hands are placed on frightening thighs. The direction is ominous, but it's clear. And every time you raise your eyes from the bar, you suffer a crisis of confidence—masked, it's true, as a spasm of disgust. *Christ. Will I really do this.* Less a rhetorical question than an admission of illness.

Sometimes we allow the perfect moment to be marred by some small wrinkle that looms disproportionately large in our minds. Example: a warm evening of stargazing from a campsite, dimmed by the glaring deer blinds mounted to the roof of a nearby pickup truck. As we mature, we realize that living more fully doesn't mean taking out the floodlights with a slingshot—a course of action that in any case would likely end with buckshot and a messy, bloody death by the campfire. Instead, we realize that living more fully means simply embracing the evening, with all its charms and flaws.

Similarly. To return to the situation before us. It would be nice to imagine that you invested the night at the penthouse wooing a perfect ten. But you didn't. Tonight you're hustling way down in the boiler room with the twos and the threes. It's not the night you were longing for, but it's the night you are in, and however ugly your companion, tonight is *always* a beautiful place to be. So embrace it.

And now that you have come to peace with your mission, we will let you in on a curious secret to the dark art of sleeping with the ugly: in its own way, it's kind of hot. Your companion's intense bedside gratitude. Your own self-debasement. It's all pretty kinky. Some people even get addicted to it.

But, to appreciate the vista, you have to summon the will to climb. For this, a cocktail definitely does not hurt. We like to avoid treating alcohol as a crutch, but this is one situation where a strong drink is simply a precondition for your good deed of the night. Make one special, scandalously ugly person happy.

Dry Gin Martini

2¾ OZ LONDON-STYLE DRY GIN (8 CL)
¾ OZ DRY VERMOUTH (2.5 CL)
2 DASHES ORANGE BITTERS (OPTIONAL)

Stir and strain into chilled cocktail glass.

Garnish with lemon peel or spear of pimiento olives.

Never out of fashion, never out of place, the martini earns every bit of its legendary status as the ultimate cocktail. In its simplicity and elegance, it shares little in common with the focus of your amorous attentions this evening. But it's a fitting choice nonetheless: the martini is an emblem of the curious mix of selflessness and hedonism that has drawn crowds to James Bond movies for generations and that you must channel to complete your mission tonight.

Let 007's sense of duty and adventure inspire you, but we respectfully disagree on his preference for shaken over stirred. Stirring a cocktail allows its subtlety to shine and keeps it from getting cloudy or over-iced. As to our recommendation for a generous ¾ ounce pour of dry vermouth, we know it's provocative. But we firmly believe that once you get to know it, you will agree that vermouth has been improperly maligned—it is an ideal modifier that transforms a glass of iced gin into a real martini. Originally, the recipe also called for a dash or two of orange bitters. This component fell to the wayside over the years, but its use in the martini is coming back into vogue as orange bitters has become more readily available. So while orange bitters is totally optional, we recommend it.

Variations

- The same rules apply for making a **vodka martini,** though the optimal proportions (as always) may turn out differently depending on what you use and personal taste.
- The **Vesper martini** is the "real" James Bond martini, the one he ordered in the 1953 novel *Casino Royale:* 3 oz dry gin *(9 cl)*, 1 oz vodka *(3 cl)*, ½ oz Lillet Blanc *(1.5 cl)*, and shake. Garnish with lemon peel.
- For a **dirty martini,** follow recipe for dry martini, adding ¼ ounce of olive brine and garnishing with olives. The brine can easily overpower the drink, so less is definitely more.
- For a **Gibson,** follow recipe for dry martini, garnishing with a spear of three pickled pearl onions. This is a welcome and overlooked alternative to the usual garnishes. And if you add a splash of the onion brine, it's a . . . oh, no.

Oh, no. *You didn't. Please, say you didn't.*

You did. Okay, listen: we understand about last night. It was late, the lighting was dim, you were feeling heroic. Under the circumstances, you did the right thing by having sex. Fine. And while you probably went beyond the call of duty by staying the night, we are generally okay with that, too. But listen: we need to be very, very clear about what happened next.

You cannot fuck ugly in the morning.

Not this person. Not after you wake up. Not again. It's not okay to do that.

If you *did* have sexual relations—in the cruel, unforgiving light of morning—you have officially gone too far. Unfortunately there's nothing you can really do about it at this point but have a drink and vow to do better next time.

> • **Dirty Gibson.** Follow the recipe for a Gibson, adding a quarter ounce of onion brine. This is a great way to have a Gibson—arguably, a splash of brine makes more sense with pickled onions than with olives, anyway.

If there isn't yet a phrase for having reprise sex with an unattractive person the morning after, "Oh, no, I pulled a *Dirty Gibson!*" pretty much wins the prize.

SECOND DATE

When you meet someone on a first date, both of you are so nervous and eager to please that neither is in a skeptical frame of mind. There is optimism in the air. You might give the person sitting beside you a free pass, scarcely stopping to notice that the picture you saw on his or her dating site profile is off by about two years and twelve pounds.

The end result is that it's the *second* impression that is make-or-break. Now is when both of you have had a few days

THE *OTHER* OTHER WHITE MEAT

GIN AND VODKA

What separates the snooty gin drinker from the slaphappy vodka guzzler? Really, just a bunch of additives. Both spirits are from grain (usually), both are typically distilled several times to create a very neutral, very potent base, and neither is barrel-aged before bottling (again, usually). What sets gin apart from vodka—and what, from a cock-tailing perspective, makes it a more interesting ingredient—is that the resulting spirit is flavored with a worldly spread of spices ("botanicals") that only an eighteenth-century imperialist could have thought up: juniper oil, coriander, citrus peels, anise, almonds, cocoa, various roots, and anything else your typical Dutch or British naturalist stomping around the teeming jungle with a waxed mustachio and a dashing pair of boots could find.

Most vodkas are charcoal-filtered and/or cut with water to smooth out the burn. If you have a playful palate and are drawn toward celebrating a spirit's unique and subtle flavors, vodka represents something of an enigma: the premium brands try and outdo one another creating as flavorless a product as possible to justify a top-shelf price. Considering all of the subtlety, craftsmanship, and tradition that you are paying for when you spring for a fancy bottle of cognac, rum, tequila, or whiskey, the craze over high-end vodka seems a little weird. All that being said, your authors have survived too many good-time vodka nights to trash the stuff. Even if it doesn't have a lot of flavor, a traditional vodka (usually made from potato, rather than grain) has plenty of body and pure fun on its side. Maybe the best vodka "cocktail" of all is to take it neat in a small glass, well chilled, with a sprawling plate of caviar and pickled fish nearby. Just like old Babushka used to take it.

to mull over each other's physical flaws, consider other available options (or the lack thereof), and brood. When you meet for your second date, you are still nervous but also maybe a bit cranky, and you have reverted to your natural, hypercritical repose. And you don't yet have an ounce of booze in your system. Ordering a drink under these conditions is fraught with peril.

The single greatest risk on a second date is contracting genital warts from someone whose name you won't remember in three months. All in all, we think that's a risk worth taking. But the *second* greatest risk is coming across like a blowhard. This is one situation where boozing plays a role that is merely facilitating and not an end in itself. You're here to *couple*, after all. Ordering anything even remotely esoteric smacks of pretentiousness. Ordering something too fruity marks you out as a lightweight. Making matters worse, this is the only part of the evening during which you're both sober: that is, simultaneously nervous and judgmental.

For all of these reasons, we recommend ordering a simple, straightforward sour like the gimlet. Then put on a smile and get your game going. Figuring out whether there will be a third date is serious work.

Modern Gimlet

2 OZ GIN OR VODKA (6 CL)
¾ OZ LIME JUICE (2.5 CL)
¾ OZ SIMPLE SYRUP (2.5 CL)

Shake and strain over fresh ice in an old-fashioned or, alternatively, up in a cocktail glass.

The recipe for a **traditional gimlet** calls for an equal pour of gin and Rose's Sweetened Lime Juice. But the advantages of fresh lime juice and simple syrup are obvious: the use of simple syrup allows you to adjust the balance of sweetness to your own taste, and freshly squeezed, properly strained juice speaks for itself. As to the use of spirit, under normal circumstances we strongly recommend this drink with gin. But for a second date, maybe you should stick with vodka, which is what most bartenders will use unless you request otherwise. With gin, you could run the risk of indicating

SOURS

The modern gimlet is in the sour family. The basic formula to remember for a sour is two parts spirit and, at most, one part each of sweet (simple syrup) and sour (strained lemon or lime juice). For the recipes you will see here, we generally recommend a bit less sweet and sour because our preference is for a drink that is more booze-forward. The inherent sweetness of your base spirit may dictate a further reduction in the amount of sweetness you use. Balance—whatever that means to you—should always be your goal.

Sours are easy to make and require only one bottle of booze to get going. And, as the many sours we recommend in this book will reveal, the derivative possibilities are endless: lemon or lime, sugar or honey, soda, egg white, egg yolk, bitters, stirred, shaken, and blended are just the beginning. You can also use a liqueur like triple sec as a sweetener instead of (or in addition to) sugar: this is sometimes called a modified or "New Orleans" sour—once referred to as a "daisy."

to your date that you take boozing as seriously as (let's face it) you do, and it's harder on the breath. Vodka does tend to go down easier, though, so make a point of sipping slowly— watch out for those STDs.

THREESOMES

The really beautiful thing about the 1980s television sitcom *Three's Company* is that it brainwashed an entire generation of boys under the age of sixteen into thinking that there was something fascinating about the sexual chemistry between a man and two women. We watched Jack Tripper with awe. Here was a man who had everything. A blonde. And a brunette. Living with him, in the same apartment. We thus received our moral instruction: Jack Tripper is very, very cool. The landlord must be stopped. Chrissy and Janet must find common ground here. This needs to happen.

Were parents back then at all concerned that their children wasted hours of their youth watching an elderly homophobic landlord lose his temper at a bunch of twenty-something tenants who acted like idiots? The answer is no. Janet and Chrissy were so wholesome and pure—how could a parent who had lived through the 1960s dare the hypocrisy of shutting this innocuous and totally vapid programming out of their home?

It's true that Jack never pulled off a threesome on *Three's Company*. And small wonder. Threesomes are difficult to manage. Everyone needs to be in the right mood, at the same time, and under the influence of the right substances. Someone needs to show the proper initiative, and run the risk of double rejection. But if it seems impossible to you, know this: every night, the moon rises over some trio, somewhere, doing something naughty with all of those moving parts. It's not only doable, it's surely being done at this very moment. So do it for love. Do it for the stories you will live to tell. Do it for Jack Tripper.

Negroni

1 OZ DRY GIN *(3 CL)*
1 OZ SWEET VERMOUTH *(3 CL)*
1 OZ CAMPARI *(3 CL)*

Stir and strain into a cocktail glass, or serve over fresh ice in an old-fashioned glass.

Garnish with orange peel.

Sweet vermouth and Campari are both traditional Old World aperitifs. Generally, aperitifs are either sweet or bitter. Which kind do you prefer? Perhaps French and Italian café denizens engaged in this kind of argument the same way youngsters of a certain era debated the relative merits of Chrissy and Janet. The Negroni doesn't ask you to choose. With aperitifs, as with sexual partners, you *can* have it both ways, and we encourage you to do so with this brilliant and iconic cocktail.

The Negroni is a nice introduction to Campari. But like any bitter, Campari is an acquired taste, and if you aren't fully onboard yet, your Negroni may want a bit less of it. Over time, we suspect your tolerance for Campari will grow and you will learn to appreciate this cocktail as it is traditionally composed, with equal parts of its three ingredients.

The Negroni is thought to have been invented by the French general Pascal Olivier Count de Negroni. Like any threesome worth the trouble, the Negroni is seductive, sensual, and complex—every bit as sybaritic as its Old World name suggests. Unsurprisingly, given its ingredients, the Negroni is a perfect overture to a satisfying meal—or, for that matter, any other satisfying ordeal you can work up with two acquaintances and a long night.

APERITIFS, PART 1

Spirits—gin, rum, whiskey, and the like—usually play the leading roles in mixed drinks. Like the actors and actresses with the biggest smiles, the most alluring buttocks, and the most markedly vapid interviews, spirits tend to dominate the conversation. But in a huge number of cocktails, an aperitif holds the supporting role. Like character actors, they aren't thought of as big box office draws. They are a little eccentric, usually short, possibly balding, and only enthusiasts know their names. But they are unquestionably talented, adapting easily to varying roles and adding maximum value to the overall product. Chief among them is vermouth.

Derived from the Latin word *aperire* ("to open"), an aperitif is traditionally used to open the palate before a big meal. Campari, amaro, and to a lesser extent Lillet (which comes in both red and white) are bitter, and in a very loose sense are used in cocktails as a flavorful, robust alternative (or addition to) bitters.

THE CLOSER

There are make or break moments in a relationship. In some relationships, it can feel like *every* moment is a make or break moment. But a real big one comes around eight weeks in. By this juncture, confidences have been made. Friends have been introduced. Family members have shared unsolicited points of view. Underwear has been removed—quite a number of times, actually—and the first box of condoms is dangerously close to empty. It's time to buy another, much bigger box of condoms, or consider a fresh prescription for birth control pills. Either way, your next visit to the pharmacy becomes, in itself, a momentous step forward in the relationship.

Unless what you really want to do is take a step backward. To take a weekend off and see how it feels. To check up on your ex, peek at newcomers to your preferred dating site—test the old waters, so to speak. In that case, your next trip to the pharmacy looms like a coffin nail, and that prescription will cost you far more than your usual twenty-dollar copay.

So: pharmacy or no pharmacy? Between you and the answer is a cocktail and a quiet evening. A . . . dare we say it? A *romantic* evening. We know it's awkward. In this day and age no one can even say "romantic" without averting their eyes. We acknowledge the existence of our emotional selves the same way we acknowledge someone passing gas: no use pretending the room doesn't smell, thanks very much, but let's move on now, shall we?

Romance, like passed gas, is slightly uncomfortable to think about. But the point of this evening—and this cocktail—is to take you out of your comfort zone. If the candles, the soft voices, the drink, and the fancy-ish clothes just feel *wrong wrong wrong*, perhaps it's time to part ways. But if there's magic in the air? Congratulations. Down your drinks with gusto, dash for your local pharmacy's "naughty" aisle, and scurry back home.

Dubonnet Cocktail

1½ oz DUBONNET *(4.5 cl)*
1½ oz DRY GIN *(4.5 cl)*

Stir and strain into a chilled cocktail glass.

Garnish with lemon peel.

Dubonnet sounds exotic, but this French aperitif (*très romantique*) is sold in most liquor stores, and a large bottle costs no more than a bottle of cheap wine. Aromatic and nicely balanced between sweet and dry, it is a fortified wine spiced with quinine, orange rind, cinnamon, chamomile flower, and other excitements. While it's a touch too intense for taking straight, Dubonnet mixes beautifully with gin, rendering a subtle and surprisingly easy-to-love cocktail.

As simple as a Dubonnet cocktail is to make, there's no getting around the fact that it's an unusual drink. But this is an unusual night. This is an elegant and, yes, romantic choice for the night that has been set aside for either closing the deal or moving on.

Variation
- The **Dubonnet Royal** is a flavorful and exciting alternative. Follow the above recipe, adding a dash of Angostura bitters, two dashes of orange or maraschino liqueur, and a dash of absinthe. This is pretty similar to what's done in the Improved cocktail (see page 160).

SELF-LOVE STILL COUNTS AS LOVE

Let's spare ourselves the details. The circumstances are clear enough and, for each of us, unique. Masturbation isn't something we learn from others. Each of us figured it out alone in a room with a latched door, using facilitating instruments of our own devising (e.g., electric toothbrush, rubber glove, mayonnaise), and so the exact procedure varies for each practitioner. Is it going too far to suggest that the ritual of masturbation is your only truly original act of creation? Possibly so. But your style of self-love is undeniably *yours*, and if all else fails, it will always be there for you. Job, home, family, car—you can lose them all. So long as you can find a generously proportioned shrub or a large cardboard box on the side of the road, a pleasant private rub will always be yours for the taking. Prison? Solitary confinement? What else is there to *do* in solitary confinement?

Whatever the reason, there may be a time when no one in the immediate vicinity is interested in having sex with you. But, fortunately, you still have your freedom, a roof over your head, a fine selection of instruments at your disposal, and a well-stocked bar. The world is yours.

Adonis

1½ OZ SWEET VERMOUTH *(4.5 CL)*
1 OZ FINO SHERRY *(3 CL)*
1 DASH ORANGE BITTERS
2 DROPS ANGOSTURA BITTERS

Stir well and strain into a cocktail or cordial glass.

Grate a small pinch of nutmeg over top
(optional).

The Adonis was invented as a tribute to a popular late nineteenth-century Broadway musical, *Adonis*, which involved a statue of the handsome and famously vain god. In the story, the statue turns human but is then disappointed with the human experience, and so reverts back to marble.

With no spirit as a base, the Adonis is perfect for a night of private play: it will loosen you up but it won't knock you down, so you will have plenty of vigor to unleash upon yourself. And it's subtle and inviting to sip, combining two classic aperitifs. The Adonis is a perfect showcase for the subtle, nutty flavors of fino sherry, which is easily obtained for a small price at any neighborhood wine shop.

Variation

- For a **Bamboo**, another classic cocktail of the late nineteenth century and equally fitting for pulling root (as it were), follow the above recipe, using dry vermouth rather than sweet.

GOING, GOING, GONE

Knowing that a relationship is on the brink of failure gives you certain license to act as an absolute shithead—precisely the shithead your significant other is increasingly convinced that you are. You leave the toilet unflushed one day, the next

APERITIFS, PART 2
FORTIFIED WINE

In France, Spain, and Italy ("where people really know how to live," as your wistful mother used to sigh), wine has for many centuries been fortified—that is, spiked with a grain or grape spirit—and sometimes aromatized for use as an aperitif.

Vermouth deserves a lifetime achievement award for its role in two great blockbusters of the cocktail world: the Manhattan (sweet vermouth) and the martini (dry). Sweet (or "Italian") vermouth is dark red in color, made from white wine, grape juice, and brandy; aromatized with a blend of herbs, roots, flowers, and bark; and sweetened with caramelized sugar. Dry (or "French") vermouth is also made from white wine, grape juice, and brandy—but it contains a different mix of botanicals, is much drier, and is white in color. Lillet and Dubonnet are additional examples of aromatized, fortified wines. Lillet is made from white Bordeaux wine and citrus liqueurs. Dubonnet is red in color, contains quinine and a secret blend of peels, spices, and herbs and is fairly balanced between sweet and dry. Try swapping in these or other fortified wines when a recipe calls for vermouth—this is an interesting area for exploration.

Sherry, a fortified (but not aromatized) wine from Jerez, Spain, finds its way into a number of really interesting, if obscure, classic cocktails. Sherry is a truly great you take a deep-tissue neck massage from your "platonic" college buddy in public, and a few hours later you use S.O.'s favorite dress shirt to detail the rims of your neighbor's pickup truck. The freedom of having nothing to lose allows you to be so much more than just a shithead. This is your chance to make passive-aggressive antics into performance art.

style of wine, unfairly overlooked in today's hard, cold world, and it's worth exploring on its own. There are a number of varieties. Most of the recipes that we mention in this book happen to call for dry sherry. Fino is driest; amontillado and Manzanilla are also quite dry. Pedro Ximénez and muscatel are sweeter but also fantastic, working well in some cocktails.

Why People Hate on Vermouth

Because fortified wine is spiked with a spirit, it will last longer than a bottle of table wine, which starts to go bad within a day or two. But even fortified wine oxidizes after it's been opened and will start to change noticeably within a week or so. Strangely, no one seems to know about this. So the likely reason so many people trash-talk vermouth is that the stuff they have tried is completely rotten. And it's true: old vermouth will destroy your cocktail. But pour half an ounce or more from a freshly opened bottle into your next martini and you will never think about vermouth in the same way again.

In light of its short shelf life, when shopping for fortified wine, buy the smallest bottle available—a small bottle of vermouth costs no more than a fast food lunch. If refrigerated, an opened bottle should last a solid month. Using a vacuum seal will give you a few weeks more.

As fun as all that is, though, it's fair to say that relationship failure presents some opportunity for self-doubt. Perhaps this particular failure was just the result of two decent but fundamentally incompatible people who exhausted all possibilities for finding common ground. But if you are solely responsible for sinking this ship, chances are high that you will soon sink another. And if you are a real piece of work—which you possibly are if you read cocktail books for self-help—you are liable to sink every ship you board. You can't know for sure whose fault it is, though, and anyway, there isn't anyone qualified to give an objective answer.

Luckily, the answer doesn't matter much. None of us really has the capacity for fundamental change, only the tendency to become feebler, fleshier versions of what we already are. You will be screwed up in pretty much the same way a year from now, pretty much no matter what else happens, unless you become an addict—which will open up a whole new range of shithead possibilities.

Worrying too much about fixing your problems will only lead you to waste time and money on a therapist whose

Tailspin

⅛ oz CAMPARI (2–3 DASHES)
1 oz DRY GIN (3 CL)
1 oz GREEN CHARTREUSE (3 CL)
1 oz SWEET VERMOUTH (3 CL)

Rinse chilled cocktail glass with Campari and discard. Stir with ice and strain into the glass.

Garnish with lemon peel.

children are more thoroughly screwed up than even you can contemplate. So save yourself the energy, the money, and the worry. For now, just embrace your inner shithead. Soon enough you will have to start impressing somebody new.

What better accompaniment for contemplating your crash-and-burn relationship than a drink called the Tailspin? Gin, chartreuse, vermouth, and Campari: four iconic ingredients to accompany your path toward redemption. Admittedly, chartreuse doesn't find its way into everyone's home. But when you do plunk down for a bottle and are raring to give it a test drive, try the Tailspin first. This is a meditative, balanced drink with layers of flavor. Glistening with subtle hues of red and green, this drink calls for, and is truly worthy of, introspection. We cannot guarantee you an unblemished romantic future. But after spending a purposeful chunk of time sipping your way through the Tailspin, there is a fair chance you will be at peace with your past.

BACK IN THE SADDLE AFTER SEVEN LONG MONTHS

Scientific research reveals that when confronted with extended periods of abstinence, your body goes through the following stages of dysfunction:

At first, your sex-starved body enjoys a false sense of security, like: *This isn't so bad. Something will come up soon, right? And we will be back on our merry way.*

At the one-month mark, complacency succumbs to a massive hormonal buildup. Drooling occurs. Fidgeting. Fist-clenching. This stage at which we can refer to as "libidinal rage" peaks some time near the ninth week and is characterized by panting on the streets as well as sex dreams, mad and wild. During this period, the frustration is so intense, celibacy seems almost kinky: you are sexless, but resolutely sexed up. Though painful, it's undeniably interesting.

After several more weeks, without any warning, desire washes lamely out of the body, like a disappointed drunk shuffling out of a forlorn whorehouse. *Nothing doing here*, it says. *This place is going downhill.* Downhill indeed: down goes your sex drive, your confidence, your attraction toward . . . toward anything, really.

Your internal life, once a fertile crescent, is now a waste-land. A nascent tyrant who has long lurked in the shadows now ascends to fill the void. It is the left side of your brain—vigorously bureaucratic, pointy-bearded, all sinew and bile—quickly learning to rule with a cold, clammy fist. All other critical organs have lapsed into a dull haze. Your executive operations become analytical, hypercritical toward every-thing around you, clenched.

As one brutal month of abstinence follows another, the left-brain dictator consolidates its power. Regional governors are replaced with regime loyalists. Discotheques are shut-tered and replaced with state party offices. Breadlines wind through grim, grimy city streets.

By the six-month mark, the dictatorship is a totally over-whelming force, morning through night. All media outlets are state-run, and they report exclusively on military dem-onstrations and the forced confessions of political dissenters whose hands are blistered from long days of grueling labor.

Seven months is a long, long time to go without love and affection. You are not a pretty sight. You are learning to hate yourself. Your friends and family find you insecure, petty, and tyrannical.

"Mr. Gorbachev!"

At the darkest hour: the defiant call of the sex deity is heard dimly, from far away, like . . . Ronald Reagan.

"Mr. Gorbachev!"

Reagan, leader of the free world, sex god! Is it him?

Even the saddest sack waiting on the longest breadline in the furthest district of the oppressed dominion hears it:

"Mr. Gorbachev! Tear down this wall!"

And when the former disco kings and queens hear Reagan's clarion call, they abandon the breadlines in droves. Who needs bread? They cast off their proletarian, ill-fitting denims and dust off their sequined pants. They head straight-away for the state-run party office, knock out the fluorescent track lighting with wooden clubs, and string up a disco ball. The left-brain dictator dies an inglorious death in his gold-plated bathroom; he was found in his deceased mother's underwear. Every citizen under forty makes mint, cruising from nightclub to nightclub in aftermarket, customized German sedans selling cocaine and real estate. The newly installed prime minister has the NATO chief on speed dial, and there are silicone implants as far as the eye can see.

When sex finally comes your way again, a Berlin Wall really *does* crumble somewhere in the psyche. You like yourself again, and everyone you know remembers why they ever put up with you in the first place. In fact, you are a hit everywhere you go.

Funky is back in town, and it's wearing new boots. Enjoy the party.

Gin Rickey

2 OZ GIN (6 CL)
1 OZ LIME JUICE, UNSTRAINED (3 CL)
CLUB SODA

Serve over plenty of ice in a highball glass,
top up with chilled club soda, and stir until the
glass frosts.

While for most drinks we recommend straining citrus juice to yield a cleaner and better-blended cocktail, the Rickey is a different beast, and it benefits from a bit of pulp. Since it isn't sweetened, this drink is a "cooler" rather than a sour. It was invented by Colonel Joe Rickey, a Confederate Army veteran whose main priority was sipping something that was sure to keep him cool in that relentless Reconstruction-era summer heat. Like any gentleman of his era raised south of the Mason-Dixon, Rickey took his drink with whiskey, but in modern times the rickey is typically served with gin. Without any sweetener—the colonel was convinced sugar heated the blood, or something—the unique qualities of whatever spirit you use are placed front and center. For this reason we recommend a fuller-bodied gin—Plymouth, ideally—that will stand up to the attention.

Whether or not there's anything to Colonel Rickey's blood-sugar theory, the gin rickey certainly is refreshing, and it *will* keep you cool: useful on hot summer days, but indispensable when your quakingly needy body is finally thrown back into action.

SEXUAL ENCOUNTERS IN GENERIC BARS
AND HOTELS ACROSS THE LAND

Sometimes you do it for love. Sometimes you are blinded by beauty. Sometimes you find yourself drawn in by the promise of poetic, athletic, tantric, sweet-Jesus-this-is-amazing sex. But sometimes, alas, you do it just because it's there for the doing. There's no love, and judging by the shape you're in, there isn't even a holdout possibility for escapades you'd want to write home about. As you order a final round, you give everything you've got to keep from toppling off the bar stool. You and the world around you are blurring and slurring, but even still it's crystal clear that: (1) not having sex is simply not an option at this point, and (2) if either one of you can even get to the finish line, it will be a heaven-sent miracle.

The inevitability, the futility of it . . . It's sort of like Greek tragedy, except instead of being poignant it's just sloppy drunken sex. God bless it. It's good for the economy. It's good for the soul. And there are some fine, decent people out there— people who donate their time to community service and their money to public radio and even forgo the free tote bag—people who would never have been born if not for the happenstance of a random sexual encounter by their parents. And you know what? Even if we're wrong about all of that—if it's bad for the economy, rotten for the soul, and only spawns the scum of the earth—it will always be good for a juicy story back home.

For better or worse, random sexual encounters *do* happen, and they tend to happen whether the setting is glamorous, picturesque, or strip-mall generic. In fact: the less impressive the environs, the better. Like a snowflake, every random sexual encounter is unique, but in ways that are so impossi-

bly insignificant that you won't notice unless you are locked
in a room at an airport motel.

Sidecar

2 OZ COGNAC *(6 CL)*
1 OZ TRIPLE SEC *(3 CL)*
¾ OZ LEMON JUICE *(2.5 CL)*

Shake and strain into a chilled cocktail glass
with a sugared or half-sugared rim (optional).

Garnish with flamed orange peel.

Like bad sex, a bad sidecar is still better than no sidecar
at all. The sidecar was not necessarily original but was an
epiphany nonetheless when it was famously served at Harry's Bar in Paris in 1930. Today, this cocktail sounds more
rarefied than it is. It follows the same proportions as another member of the extended sour family, the margarita,
with cognac replacing tequila, lemon replacing lime, and, on
the rim, sugar replacing salt. The margarita and the sidecar
are both examples of sours made in the New Orleans style,
sweetened with triple sec rather than simple syrup.

For the sidecar, a flamed orange peel will add a caramelized essence to the multiple layers of citrus already provided
by triple sec, which is flavored with sweet and bitter orange
peels. When made with care and precision, fresh juice, and
quality booze, there are few drinks more satisfying than the
sidecar tumbling through the universe.

How to Flame an Orange Peel

If sharp cutlery, citrus, and human flesh aren't adding enough excitement to your drinking life, why not involve fire? Flaming orange peel will put fear and respect into the hearts of your guests, but it has the additional benefit of adding a wonderful caramelized flavor to the drink. Use a paring knife to cut out a small silver dollar–sized dome from the orange peel, sort of like a miniature yarmulke. Light a match, pass it several times near the peel to warm up the skin, then hold the match directly over the drink and, with your other hand, squeeze the dome between thumb and forefinger so that its oils spray out toward the match and ignite over the drink. (This is why using a dome shape is important: to create a concentrated stream of oil.) We may be stating the obvious—this is really directed at your fifteen-year-old son, if you have one and if he's reading this book to prepare for a party while you are out of town—but don't do this directly in front of anyone's face. Unless you hate them.

Use the dome as a garnish.

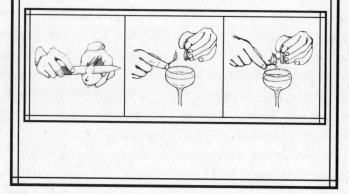

Variation

- Ordering a **Between the Sheets** before heading upstairs for anonymous sex may come across as a bit heavy-handed, or just kind of gross, like a lewd joke about the dimensions of your genitalia. But the drink is still a good one. Cut the triple sec down to ½ oz and add ½ oz of Bénédictine to fill the void. This will render a more herbaceous but equally balanced cocktail.

- Either a sidecar or a Between the Sheets can be made using an **orange curaçao** like Grand Marnier rather than triple sec.

POURING SALT ON AN OPEN WOUND, OR DRINKING WITH THE EX

You broke up sometime in the past fourteen months—maybe last week, or maybe it was exactly a year ago tonight. You have moved on, and hopefully you have had one or two more inconsequential relationships than your ex has had—somehow it matters—but in any event, all of them have fizzled. Or maybe not: maybe you are still seeing a new someone, who maybe doesn't even know that this old someone exists, and maybe you shouldn't really even be here, staring this old someone in the face, about to order a drink.

First, a question. *Why?* Why are you here?

And this is a trick question. Because if you think the answer is that you *don't* know, then you *do* know. And if you think you *do* know the answer, then your answer is wrong, whatever it happens to be. For instance, if you think that you are here to *talk*, then the answer is *sex*; and if you think the answer is *sex*, then the answer is *love*; and if you think the answer is *love*, then the answer is *talk, hate, revenge*, and, possibly, also *sex*. And, most certainly, if you think the answer is *closure*, then the answer is that you are here tonight for *explosive drama*—weeping, fireworks, rage, mea culpas—the very opposite of closure.

The real answer is that you shouldn't be here at all, but it's too late to back out now. When you make plans with an ex, you'd best be prepared to follow through and overcome whatever fears need overcoming. Which means whatever you drink should involve rum: the stuff of fearless, swashbuckling seafarers. Because let's face it, tonight you are far out at sea. And even if you think you are here for sex but are in fact here for love—that is the *worst* possible scenario, by the way—you will be more effective in getting back what you don't think you want if you are blessed, for the moment, with a sense of daring.

Old Cuban

1½ OZ AMBER RUM *(4.5 CL)*
¾ OZ LIME JUICE *(2.5 CL)*
¾ OZ SIMPLE SYRUP *(2.5 CL)*
6 MINT LEAVES
2 DASHES ANGOSTURA BITTERS
BRUT CHAMPAGNE, PROSECCO, OR OTHER SPARKLING
   WHITE WINE

Shake rum, lime juice, simple syrup, mint leaves and bitters, strain into champagne flute and top up with brut champagne or prosecco.

Garnish with 2 fresh mint leaves.

The Old Cuban isn't made with salt, but it has everything else you need for rubbing into the open wound that is your purportedly "ex" relationship: champagne, for a celebration of what was; mint, for a fresh twist on what may be; bitters, for depth and self-immolation; and rum, for causing as much destruction as possible in the time that remains. Tribute for the Old Cuban goes to Audrey Saunders, who serves it up at the Pegu Club in New York.

Variation

- For a **mojito**, use 2 oz white rum, top with club soda rather than champagne, and (for once) hold the Angostura bitters. Serve in a collins glass over fresh ice. The mojito can also be made by building the drink in the glass itself: first muddle raw sugar (rather than simple syrup) with strained lime juice or three wedges of lime, clap the mint or firmly press it against a flat surface before placing it in the glass, and then pour in the rum followed by club soda, stirring well.

THE FLING OF A LIFETIME

Who is this guy? Where has he been your whole life? And why didn't anyone tell you sex could be this good?

These are all reasonable questions, but don't expect to ever get the answers. In fact, for reasons you shouldn't think about right now and that you will probably never understand, don't even expect to get his telephone number.

If it's any consolation—and it should be—this is probably the best sex *he's* ever had in *his* life as well. That's what makes it the best. Both of you are pulling moves neither of you knew you had. These are magic moments in life, and you're blessed to have them, fleeting though they may be.

Nothing like this ever comes to earth gracefully. That's what makes it a fling. The sooner you accept that, the easier it will be to return to the world of, well, pretty good sex and dependable dates.

For now, just enjoy! Here's the perfect drink for before, after, during, and in between.

Champagne Cocktail

1 RAW SUGAR CUBE
BRUT CHAMPAGNE OR OTHER SPARLING WHITE WINE
3–4 DASHES ANGOSTURA BITTERS
1 OZ COGNAC (3 CL)

Place the sugar cube in a well-chilled champagne flute and add bitters to saturate. Add cognac and top up with brut champagne.

Nothing fuels a fling like a flute of champagne. The classic champagne cocktail is simple to make and feels fabulously decadent while you are lazing away the day in twisted-up hotel sheets.

Champagne finds its way into quite a few drink recipes, but rarely, if ever, as successfully—and famously—as it does here. Champagne and cognac are from nearly opposite regions of France, but their chemistry could almost be described as, well, sexual. If the "opposites attract" analogy goes too far for you, let's just agree that these ingredients complement each other exceptionally well.

Needless to say, the champagne cocktail is perfect for

SPARKLING WINE

Several great cocktails call for brut champagne, a sparkling white wine from the Champagne region of France. The carbonation is caused by a second round of fermentation that takes place after bottling, induced by adding yeast and sugar to the wine. Other regions around the world also create quality sparkling white wines—cava, from Spain, and prosecco, from Italy, are two examples with stellar heritages—and can serve as less expensive substitutes for champagne in many recipes. Generally you want to find something dry,

celebrations of any kind. So if you *do* happen get this guy's telephone number, maybe you can serve these up at the engagement party.

THE DRUNK DIAL

We have this idea that we plan to bank millions with. We will tell you about it, but if you steal it, we will kill you. Ready?

*Cell phone breathalyzer.**

Cell phone breathalyzer? Why, you ask? If you don't know yet, you will find out soon enough. It is a discovery that will

---

* To be perfectly honest, it turns out that LG beat us to the punch with this product in South Korea, where heavy drinking is so pervasive that it's only frowned upon when it adversely affects your karaoke skills. But South Korea also has high speed rail, incredibly cool rain boots, and universal health care. They're so far ahead they don't really count then, right?

but not austerely so. And this may come as a surprise: sparkling wine lasts for quite a long time after it's opened—say, a solid week longer than a bottle of flat table wine. A simple stopper with metal wings that clamp down can be purchased for a pittance at your local wine shop and will keep the wine from going flat (as long as it's not too close to empty). The quality of the wine is preserved thanks to those bubbles; carbon dioxide is inert and slows the oxidation process.

occur on some night that starts out quite harmlessly: you will be out and about, talking with friends, peering at the crowd, having a jolly good time. Suddenly, hormones, nostalgia, and alcohol will chemically combine to numb the part of your brain that deals in self-control. You will happen on what will seem, at the time, like a perfectly good idea: slipping discreetly outside and calling an old number buried on your contact list. You will act on this good idea, despite any resolutions you may have made before about never calling this number again. The only problem with this good idea is that it is a very, very bad idea. So why will you do it? Because drunk dialing *always* feels like a good idea at the time.

Enter the *breathalyzer*, which will deactivate your phone, thereby preventing you from reaching out to touch someone you shouldn't be touching. Brilliant! If you aren't the type to delve into your dark past when you are drinking, the cell phone breathalyzer still has its uses. As in, "I'm sorry I missed dinner and didn't come home until two a.m. And

I'm sorry I couldn't call to warn you, but you see, I failed the breathalyzer." Brilliant!

GPS, streaming video, geeky apps, *blah-blah-blah*. What

BITTERS, PART 1

Let the experts argue where and when the first cocktail was born. But wherever it was, whatever it was, that first cocktail was made with booze, sugar, water, and a healthy dash of bitters. Early bitters were developed as a remedy for nausea, and they work to that end fairly well—try a few dashes in a glass of soda water next time you feel queasy. Nearly all bitters are made from some combination of root, bark, citrus peels, and various spices and herbs. Over the years, bitters have been used to cure all manner of gastric ailments, to stave off malnutrition, and maybe even by the occasional desperate fool to cure warts—but we love bitters because of what they do for cocktails.

The truth is that we are just now emerging from the Dark Age of Bitters. There is an entire generation of boozers—say, those born between 1930 and 1965 ("Baby Boozers"?)—who by and large can't stand the stuff. Perhaps they find bitters medicinal, or the smell reminds them of Grandpa's cocktail-hour breath and his endless stories of the Great War. The more distance there is between your birth and the mid-twentieth century, the more likely you will be to fall in love with the richness, the mysterious aroma, the deepness of bitters. One whiff can evoke the rain forest, old leather, and Sweet Mama Earth herself. And adding a dash to an otherwise bland cocktail is like instant excitement, filling in for a spirit's shortcomings and amplifying its strengths.[*]

[*] Both of your authors have tried splashing bitters on family members for the same effect, but it doesn't work.

good is a smart phone if it doesn't cut off your ability to dial exes—or anyone else you shouldn't be thinking about—when you have drunk too much?

A renewed enthusiasm for bitters has played a major role in the recent (say, over the past decade) return to the classic traditions of mixology. Take the martini and the Manhattan: originally, bitters formed a critical role in the recipes for each. Since around the time the seat belt was invented (coincidence, anyone?), any bartender would look at you like you were insane if you asked for orange bitters in your martini. While getting a dash of Angostura in your Manhattan might not have been as rare, it was still something to celebrate. Even today, these ingredients are far from universally used and orange bitters in particular remain hard to find. But if you go to the right place for your nightly poison, bitters are now officially "in play."

The first bottle to purchase is **Angostura bitters**. It was developed in early nineteenth-century Venezuela by a German doctor as a means for keeping Simón Bolívar's revolutionary soldiers in good health. The precise recipe is a secret, but its primary ingredients are gentian root and angostura bark. It's highly alcoholic, but because the stuff has been around forever, it is usually exempt from regulations and available in supermarkets (you may not have noticed it before, but trust us, it's there: try the "International" aisle, whatever that's supposed to mean). Angostura is the one bottle of bitters that can be found in almost any bar. And while there is no question that different cocktails do better with other kinds of bitters, in a pinch you will usually be safe subbing in Angostura instead.

Stay tuned for the product launch. Until then, you will all be dangerously susceptible to the temptations of the drunk dial. There's nothing we can say here to convince you not to do it. Calling those old numbers is really the stupidest possible activity that you can find yourself involved with that doesn't involve getting into a car or taking off your clothes. But without a breathalyzer, you will always be at risk—so you might as well be prepared. Here are our field notes:

Nothing feels more natural than hitting the "Send" button on your phone. But with the first ring, your heart starts pounding and regret pays out in advance. After the completion of the call, you will either find yourself in a state of instant remorse and rejection (your ex's new fiancé answered the phone) or you will find yourself preparing for an exciting rendezvous. Either way, we recommend you treat yourself to a moment of pause, accompanied by one last drink before moving on to the closing chapter of your night.

Vieux Carré

- 1 OZ COGNAC (3 CL)
- 1 OZ RYE WHISKEY (3 CL)
- 1 OZ SWEET VERMOUTH (3 CL)
- 2 DASHES BÉNÉDICTINE
- 2 DASHES PEYCHAUD'S BITTERS
- 1 DASH ANGOSTURA BITTERS

Stir and strain into a cocktail glass.

Garnish with a twist of lemon.

The Vieux Carré, a 1930s classic from that bastion of mischief that is New Orleans, is a fine option for last call before ending the night with some mischief of your own. Named for New Orleans's most famous (and infamous) neighbor-hood, the Vieux Carré (French, ironically, for "old square") is an intriguing and undeniably devilish spin on the Man-hattan, with cognac sharing the main stage with rye. Pey-chaud's bitters make an appearance, because, well, Peychaud's manages to find its way into every cocktail that hails from the Big Easy.

DROWNING OUT THE TICKING OF YOUR BIOLOGICAL CLOCK

Remember those lovebirds you know who were in such a foolish rush to get married a few years back? Well, they are now expecting. And you have found yourself developing an inexplicable fascination with the baby booties you purchased as a gift for the baby shower. This is not an item that you find remotely interesting—or so you thought. But now your eyes are drawn to these little booties that sit on your kitchen counter, waiting to be wrapped. And you can't quite seem to gather the gumption to cover them in duckling-themed wrapping paper. Even though they are totally generic and were made under unfair working conditions, in the develop-ing world, they have a special, magnetic draw. They seem to be trying to tell you something. Something like, "Please don't give me away! We want to stay here, to keep *your* baby warm!"

If booties are talking to you, if you are dreaming of mile-long registries and names for your unborn children, we are here to tell you what you already know: *it's time.* Maybe it's even a quarter past time.

But don't go crazy thinking it's too late. Not even close. If you aren't in a child-ready relationship, putting pressure on yourself, your significant other, or the hottie you met twenty minutes ago at the bar is counterproductive. In fact, consider meditating on the following mantra every morning: *Ultimatums are unsexy. Ultimatums are unsexy.*

Pay attention to that biological clock. It's real. It's telling you something important. But tonight? It needs to be drowned out. Put on your best getup, hit the town, and remember that the best things happen when you are least expecting.

Bee's Knees

2 OZ GIN (6 CL)
1 OZ LEMON JUICE (3 CL)
½ OZ HONEY SYRUP (1.5 CL)

Shake and strain into a cocktail glass.

Garnish with a lemon peel or, better, a sprig of lavender or anise.

A sophisticated, light, and floral classic, the Bee's Knees is the perfect lubrication for an evening of subtle mating calls and fun for fun's sake.

This is a fairly straightforward variant of the classic sour, and it's interesting to witness how honey rather than simple syrup changes the effect, providing a mellowing counterpoint to lemon juice's acidity. Any gin will do, but a medium-bodied choice will shine. Finally, because nothing brings on the birds and the bees like the scent of spring, try steeping this cocktail with a bit of lavender or anise.

HONEY SYRUP

Honey syrup can be made simply by adding three parts honey to one part hot water. Stir the mixture until consistent and, if there's time, refrigerate before using.

FIGHTING INFIDELITY WITH INFIDELITY

A suspicious text message, an unaccountably late night, an errant hair of unfamiliar shape and color. The unmistakable redolence of naughtiness. One way or another, you discover that you have been cheated on. The revelation and its effects feel like they are happening in a whole new world, one adjacent to yours—a world that kind of sucks, and that's spewing toxic fumes over the border. It's an anti-revelation.

Even at ugly moments like these, though, you have to step back and admire sex's majestically menacing, Niagara-like power. After all, few folks actually *start* a relationship thinking that they are one day going to sleep around. Most cheaters begin with only the sincerest intentions—overshadowed, over time, by an overwhelming biological compulsion to hump (yucky word, but under the circumstances it's about right).

So recognize what's going on here: your significant other's soul was hijacked by the power of genitalia. You are just the collateral damage.

Bad as the news is, you do have options available to you. You have been victimized but are not a victim. You can walk. You can always walk! Or you can forgive. The world would be a much better place if there were more forgiveness, right? This has practical advantages. You can leverage your significant other's contrition into a stronger hand in the relationship.

Whether you walk, stay, or commit premeditated murder, there is one other thing you could do first—one act that will allow you to move forward in whichever direction with an undivided heart.

You bed her best friend. Bed his office intern. Bed a perfect stranger. Doesn't matter, really; whoever it takes to bring you redemption. Oprah, the self-help gurus, and anyone else living in a fantasy world will tell you that counter-infidelity can never bring true happiness. Maybe so. But it *will* bring revenge, which is close enough.

French 75

1½ OZ DRY GIN (4.5 CL)
¾ OZ LEMON JUICE (2.5 CL)
¾ OZ SIMPLE SYRUP (2.5 CL)
4–6 OZ BRUT CHAMPANGE (12–18 CL)

Shake and strain gin, lemon juice, and syrup into a chilled champagne flute. Top up with Brut champagne.

Garnish with lemon peel.

Some say revenge is a dish best served cold. We say revenge is a gin cocktail best served chilled, with a splash of the bubbly. Raoul Lufbery, a World War I ace pilot, claimed that the kick delivered from this boozy concoction felt like taking fire from France's trusted 75-millimeter M1897—

otherwise known as the "French 75." No wonder: of all the champagne cocktails, this one goes down with the cleanest flavor, packs the greatest punch, and instills in you the chilly grit of a top gun on a warpath for justice. And it's a pretty straightforward sour fizz, similar to a **Tom Collins,** with champagne instead of club soda. Easy to remember and to prepare.

While gin is sometimes replaced with brandy, we think gin's clean botanicals play nicely with the crispness of champagne. You may find modern recipes of the French 75 that call for less gin—but where's the fun in that? Waging war on your beloved takes fortitude. You'll need everything this old battle-ax has to give to even the score tonight.

Variations

- For a **Bitter French,** follow the above recipe and add 2 dashes of Peychaud's bitters.
- Some cocktail geeks argue that the French 75 was made with cognac rather than gin. We will stay out of the debate by just calling this a **Cognac French 75.**

TIPTOEING ACROSS THE LINE
Experimenting with Your Sexuality Is Okay

Why shouldn't a book about cocktails insert itself into the public conversation about sexual orientation? For starters, there *is* no public conversation about sexual orientation . . . or at least not a sensible one. So here's our opening shot on sexual orientation: we think it's overrated. Your sexual orientation is at best a self-fulfilling prophecy, and not a very interesting one at that. Here's how it happened: when you were thirteen years old, you stumbled on some naughty videos tucked in the back of an older sibling's dresser. You found that this or that piece of flesh—appended to this or that piece of genitalia—happened to pique your interest. Fair enough. But rather than accept the bliss of the moment and then let it pass, you felt the need (because everyone else feels the need) to append a static label to your reaction. And by staking a flag in the ground, you effectively wrote off 50 percent of the world population as off-limits for the rest of your life.

It's understandable, because damn near everyone does it. But it's boring, and lame.

Instead, we encourage our readers to reconsider what and whom they are attracted to on a moment-by-moment basis. Leave yesterday's urges behind, with yesterday's memories. See what interests you right now. See what interests you after a cocktail. See what interests you after three. Perhaps our effort at public conversation will never catch on—but that's no reason not to let the private conversation begin.

Fancy Free

2 OZ RYE WHISKEY *(6 CL)*
½ OZ MARASCHINO LIQUEUR *(1.5 CL)*
1 DASH ORANGE BITTERS

Stir with ice and strain over fresh ice in a rocks glass.

Garnish with flamed orange peel.

We agree: for a cocktail about sexual experimentation, the name "Fancy Free" is too good to be true. But so is the drink. The Fancy Free can best be understood—and remembered—as a variation on the iconic old-fashioned, substituting **maraschino**, a Balkan liqueur made from marasca cherries and their crushed pits, for simple syrup. The maraschino brings its peculiar brand of bittersweet earthiness into the mix, along with an extra dollop of 64 proof that will get you well-oiled for tiptoeing—yes, footloose and fancy-free—over to the other side.

BITTERS, PART 2

During bitters' lost decades, **orange bitters** were the varietal seemingly banished to the darkest corners of obscurity. The marginalization of orange bitters is puzzling, since they are fairly easy to get along with. Orange bitters were a standard ingredient in many cocktails in the nineteenth century that are still popular today—the dry martini chief among them—and were quietly dropped from the recipe book over the years. Orange peels, cardamom, and coriander are major ingredients. You will find that we frequently recommend orange bitters as an ingredient, but they're rarely compulsory, and in fact you will find that most cocktail books make scarce mention of them at all. If you can get your hands on some, fantastic. It will only add to what you can do. If not, never feel discouraged from making a cocktail that lists them as an ingredient because you don't have this stuff handy. Usually an extra dash of Angostura will do just fine in their absence, together with perhaps a muddled orange wheel and/or a dash of orange liqueur.

While orange bitters are rarely compulsory, they do play a critical role in the Fancy Free. If you can't get your hands on a bottle of orange bitters but you are still interested in experimenting with your, um, cocktail, then add a dash of Angostura and a dash of orange liqueur to make up for the lack.

STALKING YOUR EX

Obsession. Calvin Klein made it seem sexy, but the real thing is brutally tedious: you keep replaying the same old memories, over and over, like a worn-out cassette. You know you need to stop, but you can't. The mind keeps running, and the hands are idle. So what do you do? Reluctantly, feverishly, compulsively, you check everything there is to check—e-mail, voice mail, local news reports—for some sign that your ex is thinking about you, too. And it's pathetic, because you know the more frequently you check, the emptier your in-box seems, and every "refresh" is another strike against your self-respect.

This may go against conventional wisdom, but actually, we think obsession is a healthy emotional response to the breakup. Even unhappy relationships bind our lives together; of course splitting up leaves us unbound and, inevitably, unhinged. So why not turn your torment into a pastime that's a little more productive? If you want to know what is on your ex's mind, we recommend more, shall we say, *proactive measures.*

You might start with some garden variety electronic identity theft. First, the e-mail account. Writing out your ex's username feels strange, like slipping into someone else's undergarments. What about the password? Truthfully, it's something you've known for some time, but swore to yourself that you'd never abuse. You abuse the password. The first gush of psychic relief washes over you. *This feels so right,* you think. You check the in-box for e-mails of interest. You check the sent mail for e-mails of interest. You linger over a few old correspondences between you, from way back when you were a happy couple—back when your ex was neither a "self-delusional psychopath" (to quote your parting words, seven weeks ago) nor a victim of identity theft.

Once you have violated the veil of privacy, what's the point in stopping, really? Credit card charges, bank account balances, cell phone records, and more are all suddenly available for thoughtful review. You are free to follow the money trail wherever it will take you, to exciting items of interest like extravagant dinner tabs, recklessly late cab rides—*the kinds of cab rides where things happen in the backseat*—pharmacy charges.

You have now acquired information. You have begun to assemble a narrative. But more important, your blood is pumping, and you feel productive. You are truly alive for the first time in weeks. And it's all been quite cathartic. Your good side has awoken, and now acknowledges that perhaps it's time to move on with your life.

Or perhaps it's time to surrender fully to your need for knowledge, your spicier side declares. *Your need for more items of interest.* Your dull side goes back to sleep, and the work continues. The Internet, even with its prodigious depth, has yielded all it can yield. Now it's time for the real work to begin. Black hoodie—check. Ninja slippers—check. Nightvision goggles—check. Bionic ear—check. Poisoned blow darts—check.

You may find yourself hidden in the shrubs. You may find yourself jimmying a dark window, your tall and sinister shadow working feverishly alongside you. You may find yourself inside a home, with its familiar smell and quality of light. You may find yourself looking for various items of interest. You may find yourself relaxing on the couch. You may find yourself slipping into . . . well, those undergarments we spoke about before. You may find yourself in bed, "cozy." You may find yourself happy, very, very happy. You may find yourself waiting. Waiting for a very long time.

No doubt this is a story with a happy ending—who doesn't enjoy coming home to their ex squatting in a dark corner wearing stolen underwear and night-vision goggles, aiming a poison dart at the door, with letters and other items of interest strewn about? But we'll leave the night's conclusion for you and your ex to resolve, with just one observation: with all that waiting around, you will get thirsty, and there's always the liquor cabinet to explore.

Pisco Sour

2 OZ PISCO BRANDY (6 CL)
¾ OZ SIMPLE SYRUP (2.5 CL)
¾ OZ LEMON JUICE (2.5 CL)
½ OZ EGG WHITE (1.5 CL)
3 DROPS FEE'S OLD FASHION OR ANOSTURA BITTERS

Shake pisco, simple syrup, lemon juice, and egg white without ice to foam, then with ice to chill.

Strain into a cocktail glass.

Dash Fee's Old Fashion or Angostura bitters (if your ex has either on hand)—otherwise, use perfume/cologne—into a jigger or small cup and twist it over the top of the drink, creating a thin stripe over the drink's foam.

Pisco, an unaged brandy made from grapes grown in the deserts of South America, is a fitting brew for the forlorn and the desperate. It's also perfectly suited for a classic sour. Remember that the general guideline for the sour cocktail family is as easy to remember as the combination on your ex's padlock: two parts spirit, one part sweet, and one part sour. Because we prefer our sours a bit more spirit-forward, our recipe for the pisco sour is consistent with our other sour recommendations: ¾ ounce (rather than a full ounce) of lemon juice and simple syrup each. But you are encouraged to experiment with measurements that work best for you.

Pisco's rough edges are smoothed out by the texture and flavor of egg white. Egg white can be used in many sours, but if you are afraid to go there, it's never compulsory. Unlike most other members of the sour family, the pisco sour enjoys the added dimension of a dash of bitters, particularly one with a noticeable cinnamon aroma like Fee's Old Fashion. But use whatever you can find; a sour with a dash of bitterness is what stalking your ex is all about.

Variation

- If you can't get your hands on pisco, try making a **tequila sour** in the same style. On the surface, agave and the pisco grape share little in common: one is something like a cactus, the other is a fruit. But in flavor and aroma, tequila and pisco are closer than you would expect—perhaps because both are grown in the desert and so share a common *terroir*.

> ### Egg White
>
> To extract an **egg white**, crack the egg in half but keep it cradled together over the drink, allowing the white to pour out and the yolk to remain in the shell. Feed the yolk to your dog for healthy, shiny fur.

EMOTIONALLY UNHEALTHY MOMENTS IN BEAUTIFUL PLACES

You are with two traveling companions in a softly lit, casual bar on a cobblestone street, perhaps overlooking a quiet fishing port in Colombia or a hillside in Liguria, or tucked behind the Rue du Bac in Paris. Miraculously, there are no other tourists. The people around you are simply living their lives—so casually, effortlessly, without sufficient appreciation for the sheer beauty that surrounds them. You think: *what did I do wrong in my past life that I don't live here?* The hard truth is that the reason you don't live here has nothing to do with your past life and everything to do with what you're doing wrong in *this* life. But you still you have a chance to make things right.

So let's discuss your traveling companions. They are both attractive. Perhaps they are from the place you are traveling to, or a country nearby. You are in love with the one with the strong, determined brow—sick with love. Why else would you end up in this absurd situation, wasting your travel time mired in a dithering, platonic stew? So far, it has not yet worked out to your advantage, and if you are honest with yourself, you know that it never will.

You have two options. You can keep trying for the one with the fine brow. You may even get lucky, if everyone drinks enough and timing and happenstance work in your favor. But regardless of the outcome, what will be left of your dignity if you keep at it with the puppy-dog routine?

You have been ignoring the second option, also attractive and with slender hands, for no good reason other than that this person has a significant other somewhere else, far away, whom you have never met. In other words, what stands between you and Slender Hands is an abstract barrier that can easily be dispensed with—by ignoring it.

We are not suggesting that you lower your sights. We are informing you that all of this has nothing to do with love and everything to do with power. The only way to extract yourself with your self-respect intact is to ignore Fine Brow, charm the one that's hitched, and close the deal. Try to have sex with Slender Hands within earshot of Fine Brow. Then ditch them both shortly after, circle back to town in a few days, find a cheap short-term rental, and spend several hundred hours in this café, with or without a lover—but with resolve in your heart and peace in your loins.

Death in the Afternoon

¾ OZ ABSINTHE (2.5 CL)
BRUT CHAMPAGNE

Top up with Brut champagne.

Build in a thoroughly chilled champagne flute.

Is there anyone more qualified than Hemingway to steer us toward the proper drink for this tragic and picturesque scene? Ten years ago the Death in the Afternoon, famously invented by the great Papa when stranded on a beached fishing boat for seven hours in 1935, was mere legend. Mixologists sometimes referred to it as the "Near Death" when made with a pastis, which is similar to absinthe except that it lacks that most mythical of ingredients: real, honest-to-goodness, hallucinate-on-the-dance-floor-in-Prague wormwood. Thanks to the relegalization of absinthe (bitterer than pastis, but dance floor hallucinations are, in truth, not included), we are enjoying a renaissance in absinthe-based cocktails. Death in the Afternoon is a prime example.

Absinthe, pastis, ouzo, sambuca, raki: close cousins that have formed a pillar of boozing for anyone living within marching distance of the Mediterranean since the rise of Byzantium. But the strong anise flavor (or in some cases licorice, which is slightly different) can be a bitter pill for the uninitiated.

The original Death in the Afternoon called for a full 1½ ounces of absinthe. Since absinthe can run as high as 144 proof, this yields an extremely powerful drink—it was called "Death" for a reason—and many people (including us) will find that half as much absinthe will yield a more balanced, less destructive drink.

SMOLDERING JEALOUSY IS THE STIFFEST DRINK

It's nice to be the most attractive person in the room. It's a guilty pleasure. But tonight, regrettably, that guilt is not yours to enjoy. It's someone else's. Who is she? Why can't

ABSINTHE

Absinthe presents a very intense anise flavor, is quite bitter, and has a very high alcohol content. It was banned virtually worldwide shortly before Prohibition due to a widespread belief that it drove people crazy. It is true that absinthe is made partly from wormwood, which contains the psychoactive chemical thujone. But thujone's final concentration in absinthe appears to be far too low—and was probably even far too low way back when Van Gogh was sipping it—to warrant much fuss. After barely surviving this century-long smear campaign, absinthe is legal again.

Here's where the fuss is warranted: absinthe plays a critical role in many of the most impressive cocktails. The Sazerac, the Improved, and Death in the Afternoon, to name just a few, are sublime and aren't possible without absinthe. Because absinthe's flavors are so intense, for many recipes a dash or a rinse is all you need to enliven a drink in a very special way.

The traditional way to enjoy absinthe is to place a sugar cube onto a perforated spoon and hold it over a glass containing an ounce or two of absinthe, then trickle cold water over the sugar, which will slowly melt into the glass, sweetening and diluting the absinthe. Whatever you use to dilute the absinthe, it will cloud—or *louche* (pronounced like "gauche")—as the ingredients mix. It's a visually appealing, almost seductive process that is closely associated with the ritual of enjoying absinthe. In addition, diluting absinthe is necessary to release its essential oils; it's far too concentrated to enjoy neat.

There are a number of new absinthes now on the market, of varying degrees of quality—though they aren't supposed to contain any thujone. **Pernod** was the first company to bottle absinthe in the eighteenth century, and they are back at it now with one of the better offerings on the market.

she leave? Why do everyone's eyes keep flitting over to that side of the room, and can you go home now?

But just as you are settling into the idea of enjoying the evening on its own terms, the world gives way beneath you, *twice*. The revelations are bad—so bad you are surprised at the limits of your imagination, because you couldn't conceive of bad quite like this.

The first revelation: this miracle of the human race happens to be standing next to your ex.

This is dismaying to say the least. Have you enjoyed your freedom? Indeed you have. The sensation of not dealing with someone else's emotional baggage has felt nothing less than exhilarating. For some time now you have wondered pleasantly how you will ever readjust to the monotony of a relationship. And all of this freedom has agreed with you rather nicely, until this very moment.

You sidle up to the loathsome couple and pretend, in a composed sort of way, to act surprised by their presence. After exchanging meaningless pleasantries (a forlorn ex-mating call of sorts), here comes the second revelation: they are engaged.

You blink a long, single blink—the kind of blink that is ineffective as a cure against vertigo—and when your eyes open, your life is in shambles. Maybe it should have no impact on your life that a fundamentally rotten person you once knew is now bound to another person who is probably just as rotten. Probably it shouldn't matter. But it's nothing less than devastating.

Goddamn it. Is it just that she's attractive? This doesn't quite describe it, since the word "attractive" suddenly seems drained of objective content. Right now, "attractive" is a purely relative term: it only has meaning relative to . . . (Walk back to your side of the room now. Take a sip of your drink.) Relative to *you*.

Advising that this is not a moment worthy of self-reflection would be kind, but insincere. So let's be sincere, and hurtful. The reason that all of this is killing you is because in fact it reflects poorly on you. It highlights a failure in your past, and because your love life is going approximately nowhere these days, hints at a failure in your present. It's a reminder that you are capable of misjudgment and possibly incapable of participating in a functional relationship. In all likelihood you are not as good at oral sex, tennis, or conversation as your replacement. You clearly aren't as attractive, you are almost certainly poorer, and you are definitely older.

It's lovely to contemplate that each of us is special and amazing in our own way. But just as surely, each of us is mediocre in our own way, and each of us is especially mediocre when compared to some other person out there in the world—a person with our precise interests and abilities, and far more talent. A person who just may be engaged to your ex. (Sorry about that.)

But there may be some redemption here. Though the angel-face standing by the devil may be, in the most superficial sense, an undeserved upgrade, there is always the outside chance that this universe is governed, after all, by a benevolent higher power. Maybe it so happened that Ms. Perfect communicated to your ex a painful and visually conspicuous STD. And maybe a few months from now—a period that could possibly be characterized by open sores and agonizing rash—the two of them will get hit by a bus while walking out of a health clinic. You never know.

Whiskey Sour

2 OZ BOURBON OR RYE WHISKEY (6 CL)
¾ OZ LEMON JUICE (2.5 CL)
¾ OZ SIMPLE SYRUP (2.5 CL)
½ OZ EGG WHITE (OPTIONAL) (1.5 CL)

If using an egg white (for a smoother edge and a nice froth), shake without ice to foam, then with ice to chill.

Serve over fresh ice in an old-fashioned glass.

Garnish with lemon wedge and a cured or maraschino cherry.

Are we being too literal in recommending this patriarch of the sour family as a remedy for a case of sour grapes? Not at all. If you ever find yourself stuck in the kind of hellish room where jealousy and lust are ricocheting around like Ping-Pong balls, the classic whiskey sour bestows a dollop of quiet confidence. And the whiskey smash, a minty derivative, is a sure way to turn up the dial on your inner joy.

P.S.: If there *is* a higher power, your ex may or may not contract a disease and get hit by a bus. But you are definitely going to hell.

Variation

• For a **whiskey smash**, firmly press 5–6 mint leaves against a flat surface, or give them a good, hard clap, then place into glass before pouring drink. Garnish with lemon wedge; leave out the egg white and the cherry.

MUDDLING

Some bartenders like to use fine sugar rather than simple syrup when muddling citrus, since the granules will abrade the skin of the lime and release the citrus oils. For mint leaves, though, we don't recommend the kind of athletic, almost psychopathically vigorous muddling—sleeves rolled up, biceps pulsing, teeth gnashing—you may have witnessed in the past. Shredded leaves are nice in a salad but in a drink they stick to the teeth, clog up at the lip of the glass, release an unpleasant bitterness, and generally wreak havoc. We think that clapping or firmly pressing the leaves before setting them in the drink with a quick stir is just as effective in releasing the mint's fragrance. Alternatively, you can shake the mint leaves with other ingredients, strain them out with the ice, and then garnish with fresh leaves.

Stage 2

Sometimes
We Drink

and

Don't Think
About Sex

DRINKING ALONE

Of all the situations that call for a drink, this is one that deserves a book of its own. Psychopaths, depressives, young women, old men, social butterflies, prowlers, writers, ski-bums, heads of state, CEOs, workaholics, and plain old alcoholics each have their own great reasons to be drinking in the company of no one else—and we celebrate them all. As deplorable as it is that a certain stigma has attached to the pastime over recent years, the dedicated among us remain undeterred.

Drinking with other people is fine enough. But what was it again that occurred to you last time you shared a drink with a friend? On your way home, you developed a theory about Other People. A big theory—it may be hard to remember in all of its intricacy. *Oh, right.* Here it is:

Other People Suck.

Unpacking the word "suck" in this context is really where your grand theory's complexity lies, but the headline gives us reason enough to conclude that one thing we should always be when drinking alone is *content*.

So whenever it's time for you to settle down to a drink on your own-some, open your heart to the cocktail of contentment and enjoy the company of your oldest companion: your own sweet, misunderstood, and—you know what?—goddamn-near-perfect soul.

American Whiskey

Whiskey is a grain alcohol aged in oak barrels. Originally, **rye** was the big shot in cocktailing—it was the primary ingredient in both the Manhattan and the old-fashioned, and is usually called for in a Sazerac—and it's making a huge comeback these days. Rye is spicy and dry and made from, well, mostly rye. It's a little severe for drinking straight but it definitely pulls its weight in a cocktail. At some point in the middle of the twentieth century, rye lost serious ground to **bourbon**, which is made predominantly from corn, and is frequently (though not always) far sweeter than rye. Most recipes that originally called for rye are now thought of as bourbon drinks—but again, over the past five or six years rye has started to rebound.

We aren't playing favorites here; both bourbon and rye are capable of hanging with the best of the Old World spirits, and both are very much worth mixing into cocktails. You may find that mixing with bourbon will require a more modest dash of sugar or simple syrup than if you use rye. It's worth noting that rye was probably the early cocktailer's favorite because rye (the grain) was grown in the East, close to New York, where most cocktails were developed. It was also quite common in New Orleans, another hotbed of refined boozing. Bourbon was a mostly southern, rural hootch. But we are all one big urban-sprawl nation now, so use whatever you can get your hands on and leave the rye vs. bourbon dispute to the Hatfields and McCoys.

If you are wondering where the big Jack Daniel's fits into all of this, it's technically neither a bourbon nor a rye, but rather a **Tennessee whiskey.** Tennessee whiskeys go through a unique charcoal-filtering process but are otherwise similar to bourbons.

Perfect Manhattan

2¼ OZ BOURBON OR RYE WHISKEY (6.5 CL)
½ OZ DRY VERMOUTH (1.5 CL)
½ OZ SWEET VERMOUTH (1.5 CL)
LONG DASH ANGOSTURA BITTERS

Stir with ice and strain into a chilled cocktail glass.

Garnish with lemon peel.

Of all the spirits that find their way into cocktails, whiskey is the most fascinating, at once obscure and alluring. There are so many different kinds of whiskey from so many different parts of the world, and they vary tremendously in style and taste. What's more, even whiskeys that hail from the same region and are made in the same style can be dramatically different from one another. Consequently, even though the Manhattan can be made only from rye or bourbon, it can turn into a wildly different beast depending on which one you use. And precisely how much vermouth and bitters you will want to use depends greatly on your choice of spirit.

"Perfect" isn't used here to suggest that this is an objectively "perfect" Manhattan. Rather, a "perfect" cocktail is any one that calls for equal parts dry and sweet vermouth. A traditional Manhattan softens whiskey's bite exclusively with sweet vermouth's rounder, fruitier qualities. It's a fantastic drink, in some ways really the ultimate cocktail, and we heartily recommend it. But making room for a measure of dry vermouth, as we do here with our recipe for the Perfect Manhattan, will deliver a crisper, floral quality into the mix. The combination of the two fortified wines, when properly balanced, can contribute to a sublime drink, layered beautifully and faceted like a gem. And that, right there, captures the value of drinking alone: an opportunity to muse on life's mysterious balance, its fleeting charms, its tormenting flashes of perfection. Or something.

Variation

- For a **traditional Manhattan,** omit the dry vermouth and use a full ounce of sweet vermouth instead: 2¼ oz bourbon or rye, 1 oz sweet vermouth, 1 dash bitters.

OUTDOOR BARS

That first Friday in June. Is there anything better? It's the day of the year when you stop wondering why you never moved to California, and you start thinking: this is what winter is for. For the joy that reverberates through an amazingly beautiful late spring afternoon, through birds and flowering trees and shining faces and through the stack of summer weekends piled in front of you like hundred-dollar bills. It's a nearly hormonal buzz and, to our readers who live in a perfect climate year-round, sorry: this kind of euphoria is only possible after months of excruciating misery. Isn't that the East Coast ethic, after all? Suffer and cuss, lift off into bliss for a few months, then suffer and cuss all over again.

So: minds drawn to longer days, lovelier nights, and the birds and the bees. The blood is pumping through the veins. Sweet Lord, it's time for a cocktail, near the beach, on a front porch, or at a tree-shaded street corner. Time to just Take. It. All. In. Specifically, take in all those beautiful people passing by—who have been exactly where since last August? Perhaps they stay inside doing crunches all winter. Or maybe they are part of some sex-fueled winged migration that arrives from Miami with the goldfinches when the weather gets warm.

As for the cocktail, this is one you don't need our help to figure out. You were born knowing this. The summer has just begun, youth is still nigh, and there is time for everything under the sun. What else could you possibly drink?

Margarita

2 oz white tequila (6 cl)
¾ oz lime juice (2.5 cl)
¾ oz triple sec (2.5 cl)
1 dash simple syrup (optional)

Shake and serve over fresh ice in a cocktail or margarita glass (salted rim optional).

What says springtime like daisies? And, if you are in a Mexican frame of mind, what says daisy like margarita? Nothing, really, because "margarita" is, in fact, Spanish for "daisy." Fittingly, the margarita owes its existence to the early twentieth-century American vacationers who took their love of the daisy—a sour made with a traditional spirit (gin, cognac, rum, or whiskey), orange liqueur, and lemon juice—vacationing to Mexico. Apparently the forefathers of Señor Frog's knew how to entertain the gringos even back then. They started with the popular daisy and Mexified it with the local ingredients: tequila and lime. Mix it all together and you get a cocktail that screams "mellow joy" in English, French, Swahili, and every other language that has a word for springtime.

If you walk into a supermarket and look at the seventy-five hyphenated ingredients listed on the back of a bottle of margarita mix, you would think this was something terribly complex to make. Not so. A world-class margarita is made with freshly squeezed lime juice, a lick of salt, and two kinds of booze. It doesn't get any easier, tastier, or more joyful than that.

LIQUEURS

Cocktails became more complicated beasts when American bartenders gained access to imported products from Europe. These exotic liqueurs and aperitifs were not carefully crafted by Italians, French, and the like for the purpose of dumping callously into a glass with whiskey and ice. But Americans, classy and restrained as ever, started using sweetened liqueurs instead of (or in addition to) sugar, and herbal liqueurs and aperitifs instead of (or in addition to) bitters. So as a historical matter and for your own purposes, liqueurs and aperitifs should be understood as expanding the range of flavors that can be rendered out of a cocktail. We know: it's hard to pay fifty dollars for a bottle of some weird stuff wrapped in straw that you never even noticed before. But your drink options are really limited if, for instance, you don't have at least one bottle of quality orange liqueur.

Orange liqueur: many recipes call for **triple sec,** a grain spirit flavored with different varietals of exotic orange peels. The original and arguably the finest is **Cointreau.** There are several other good options, but the cheaper stuff tends to be cloyingly sweet and will mess up your drink.

Variation

- For a **rum daisy**, follow the above recipe using rum rather than tequila and lemon juice rather than lime. A dash of club soda can never hurt and is probably closer to the traditional concoction served up at Abuelo Frog's way back when.

Orange curaçao is also a sweet, orange-flavored liqueur, but because it's made with brandy rather than a neutral grain spirit, it is fuller-bodied than triple sec. **Grand Marnier**, made with cognac, holds title as the premium brand here. While orange curaçao doesn't come up as frequently in modern recipes as triple sec, we do recommend it as an interesting and worthwhile substitute. Grand Marnier, for instance, will do swimmingly with heavier spirits, as in a **sidecar** (paired, fittingly, with cognac) or a nontraditional margarita made with aged tequila. It may prove overpowering if paired with a white spirit, unless bitters are involved (as in the **Pegu Club**).

Other sweet liqueurs include **maraschino** (marasca cherry), **Drambuie** (Scotch-based, flavored with honey), **crème de cassis** (black currant), **crème de cacao** (cocoa), **coffee** (as in Kahlúa), and **crème de menthe** (mint).

Chartreuse and **Bénédictine** are both herbal cordials with ancient beginnings—both, in fact, invented in monasteries. Each adds a unique flavor component really like nothing else, critical to some of the more intriguing classic cocktails.

SWEET LORD, WHY IS EVERYONE HERE SO HOMELY?

A night out on the town does not come cheap. Expenses add up, plus there is hell to pay in the morning. Is it fair to say that you put your heart and soul into making the most of it? Yes, it is fair to say. And it isn't asking too much, is it, to expect that others put their best into it, too? All those other people filling the bar: you expect them to respect the evening. Look happy and shallow. Or look brooding and sexy. Embody anything, other than mediocrity. Bring magic to the evening.

It's shameful—criminally so—when other people choose to be ugly on your night out. If they can't simply choose to be more attractive, perhaps they can choose to be elsewhere? Is this *really* what it has to mean to live in a free country?

Well, yes, suffering the homely is *exactly* what it means to live in a free country, unless you happen to live in Miami, certain zip codes of Los Angeles, or lower Manhattan. Meanwhile, if the lords of the cocktail care an ounce for suffering, shallow souls like you, they would have invent a suitable concoction for whiling away a hard-earned evening with so many pitifully poor lookers. Fortunately, they did.

American Beauty

1 OZ COGNAC (3 CL)
1 OZ DRY VERMOUTH (3 CL)
1 OZ ORANGE JUICE (3 CL)
2–3 DASHES GRENADINE
2–3 DASHES SIMPLE SYRUP

Shake and strain into a cocktail glass.

Garnish with well-rinsed rose petal (optional).

Flip the script and enjoy this classic beauty, whose balance and sophistication will stimulate your mind and distract you from the homely masses. You can only stare into the mirror and thrive on your own self-confidence for so long, so order up an American Beauty and revel in your drink instead. With only a solitary ounce of hard liquor and another ounce of Sunday school orange juice, the American Beauty is not as booze-forward as most of the other drinks you will find in these pages. But just as well. Better you should keep your wits about you and make it out of here alone.

BRUNCH

The Bloody. We love it. Like barbecue, it's an American gastronomical passion we can all be proud of and, unlike barbecue—no disrespect here—the Bloody doesn't involve hacked-up animal parts, lighter fluid, or carcinogens. Bloodies are fun to talk about, more fun to make, and really fun to drink.

We could try to be original and come up with some other cocktail you should be imbibing to wash down the bacon. With your liver still pumping through last night's toxins, we could pry into why you feel the need to take a cocktail with your breakfast at all. And it's true that the kind of person who brunches regularly is the kind of person who has given up any pretense of anything approaching prudence or moderation. Fortunately, the Bloody is the one drink you can have at breakfast without feeling judged. (Don't even think the word **mimosa**. You think if there's a Fox News correspondent sitting at the adjacent table, she won't skewer you for swilling brut champagne in the morning?)

Morning is no time to be a contrarian about selecting

your drink. Truthfully it's not the wisest time to be drinking at all—but too late now. Just pour yourself a good Bloody, get to work on that heaving slab of carbohydrate-rich French toast, and, while you're at it, give that Fox News correspondent a piece of your mind.

Bloody Maria

2 OZ TEQUILA (6 CL)
4 OZ TOMATO JUICE (12 CL)
LEMON JUICE TO TASTE
BLACK PEPPER TO TASTE
CELERY SALT TO TASTE
HORSERADISH PASTE TO TASTE
WORCESTERSHIRE SAUCE TO TASTE
CHILE SAUCE TO TASTE
OLIVE BRINE TO TASTE

Build in an ice-filled collins glass and stir briefly.

Garnish with lemon wedge, olive, and celery stalk.

Bloody *Maria*, you say? After all our talk about taking the straight and narrow, we abandoned blond-haired, blue-eyed vodka for saucier, south-of-the-border tequila? Of course you can always stick with vodka if you wish—it's how the drink was originally conceived. But swapping in tequila, in addition to providing some additional excitement to your morning, has a way of pulling together all of those disparate ingredients into something more memorable. It's a far more dynamic spirit, and its unique vegetal bite works beautifully with tomato juice.

Variations and an Alternative

- A **Bloody Mary** is made with vodka.
- A **Red Snapper** is made with gin and works very well.
- Accompanying the gin version with a splash of clam juice renders a **Bloody Caesar.**
- For the suspiciously effete **mimosa,** pour 2 oz chilled, freshly squeezed orange juice and top with brut champagne. Serve in flute.

A DRINK WITH OLD FRIENDS

Our oldest friendships provide us a critical service. Call it grounding therapy. How far you have come in the world is, in another light, how far you have strayed. Sitting down with the original clan snaps you right back down to earth, and can put you more in touch with who you really are than a year of meditation in the Himalayas. In a minute or less, it becomes crystal clear that all the stuff you checked at the door—your job title, your zip code, your well-stamped passport—is secondary to your identity.

Do you want to know the truth about this book? It's buried right here, deep in the middle, where our editor won't find it:

The truth is that the right drink for right now isn't necessarily this cocktail or that cocktail. The right drink is always, always, *always* whatever you bloody well feel like drinking. You don't win any points in this world for ordering a mint julep at the horse races. You win points for betting on the right horse. But win or lose, trying new drinks is fun. We wrote this book to give you a few more ideas, and, while we were at it, to give you some suggestions about when to try them.

We are making this point now because your oldest friends will be the first to dress you down if you try and pull any bullshit with your drink order. Putting on airs will always catch up with you sooner or later, but with old friends it will catch up with you as soon as the words "Mary Pickford" come out of your mouth (not that it's a bad drink . . . far from it: see page 105).

If hanging out with old friends is all about going back to the basics, we recommend sitting down to a long night of gin and tonics. Like your original gang and that story about your tenth-grade teacher finding urine in her coffee mug, the gin and tonic is the kind of thing that never gets old. And whenever you have had the first in a long while, you will always find yourself wondering why you ever sat down with anything else.

Gin and Tonic

2 OZ DRY GIN (6 CL)
TONIC WATER

Build in an ice-filled highball glass. Top up with tonic.

Garnish with lime wedge and stir briefly.

While tonight is all about honoring your formative experiences, you will be well-served to avoid that cheap well gin you drank with this same crew back in the good old days. A classic dry, London-style gin (Beefeater comes most readily to mind, but is far from the only option) holds up beautifully with tonic and embodies the sort of timeless, stalwart loyalty that is the very bedrock of the perennial get-together.

Bottled tonic water is always better than what passes for tonic out of a soda gun—both because the bottled stuff is fizzier and because the flavor is not tainted with the other six liquids that emanate out of the soda gun's single orifice. Tonic is both bitter (quinine) and sweet (sugar)—making the gin and tonic, despite its uneven reputation, a fairly classic cocktail.

SUFFERING THROUGH SPORTS

Love is a give-and-take business. When you are in a serious relationship—on the road to mortgages, joint tax returns, and spawn—there is going to be some stuff you will, one day, want to take away from each other. It's okay to expect a little friction along the way. Anyway, who can respect a partner who doesn't have some misgivings about surrendering their freedom? The best way to plan for those dicey days when sacrifices are requested and resistance is expected is to build up a whole lot of good will as early as possible in the relationship.

We hope this doesn't come off sounding regressive. We are conscious that there will be readers who feel that our perspective is dated. But nothing tells a man that you are on his side like a cheery willingness to suffer through an afternoon of high-definition sports television and unwashed pals.

Repetitive jokes, cases of beer, muddy shoes, and pointless arguments about statistics: the whole bit. Just tell yourself that it's all worth it—even after you find those chicken bones one of his friends will inevitably lose behind the couch. You are putting money in the bank. One day, when you are lost in a maze of Wal-Mart aisles dedicated exclusively to those stupid toys that dangle from baby car seat handles, or when you are debating how an upright mixer could possibly be worth over $400, you will have the memory of this painful afternoon to summon on your behalf.

So what to drink? Well, the boys will be drinking beer, there's no doubt about that. You can always join in. But since you're throwing away your day, you might as well impress the hell out of his friends, and nothing impresses like a woman who knows how to mix a cocktail. Plus, if you are drinking your own cocktails, that means more beer for them.

He may not know it, his friends may not know it, but *we* know it: your boyfriend made a deal with the devil today. Isn't it fitting, then, to drink El Diablo?

El Diablo

1½ OZ REPOSADO TEQUILA *(4.5 CL)*
½ OZ CRÈME DE CASSIS (CHAMBORD IN A PINCH) *(1.5 CL)*
½ OZ LIME JUICE *(1.5 CL)*
GINGER BEER

Shake and strain into a collins glass and top up with ginger beer.

El Diablo is from a breed of modern classics based on tequila. Tequila isn't found in many traditional recipes—it wasn't on the nineteenth-century barman's shelf—but its spicy and vegetal qualities render a totally unique and surprisingly easy-to-drink concoction. A balanced tequila recipe, like this one, will put to rest the memory of those ulcer-inducing bar shots you had last New Year's. A reposado tequila should be used to round out the spicy punch of the ginger beer, and together they will stand up admirably to those spicy chicken wings you will be digging into all afternoon.

To make a strong visual impression, try dripping the crème de cassis slowly down a spiraled barspoon handle into the base of the glass. If you are incredibly bored and in desperate need of distraction, use a citrus press to squeeze out the lime juice. Then place the inverted lime shell on top of the drink as a float, with an extra splash of crème de cassis inside. This will keep you entertained—and will send everyone else in the room home wondering how their friend lucked out with a woman who knows how to float shots on top of her cocktails.

TEQUILA

Tequila is distilled from fermented agave nectar. Contrary to popular belief, agave isn't a cactus—it's actually related to the lily—but it is grown in the desert. In order from light to dark, tequila can be: plata or blanco (silver, or white, bottled within sixty days of distillation), reposado (aged between two months and a year in oak), añejo (aged more than a year), or extra añejo (aged more than three years). El Diablo is an example of a cocktail that calls specifically for the medium-bodied reposado. The margarita is traditionally made with white tequila.

BARBECUES

What's the point of it all?

It's a fair question that has been asked for millennia by the stressed-out, the hapless, the idle, and the philosophic.

And in a world in which Jimmy Fallon gets his own late-night show while we toil away at our day jobs, it's never been a more poignant question. We don't have all the answers in life and we certainly can't explain what Jimmy Fallon ever did to deserve fame and fortune. But we do know something about the connection between existential crisis and barbecue.

While scientists believe that seasonal affective disorder is caused by reduced exposure to sunlight, we suspect it has something to do with reduced exposure to cooking with fire. Sizzling prime cuts, sausage, chicken thighs, zucchini, eggplant, bell peppers, and kale on a hot grill at dusk bring happiness to humankind—plain and simple. Ribs slow-cooking through a long afternoon pour forth a smoke shamanistic in power. Barbecue's magic, like that of drinking, is of equal force whether you are all alone or at the party of a lifetime.

RUM

Rum is distilled from sugarcane juice and/or molasses—basically the sludge left over after you extract crystallized sugar. This spirit has played an outsized role in New World history. The Boston Tea Party was about more than just tea (would people really risk their lives for tea?), and rum unfortunately played a critical role in the economics of the slave trade as well. Recently, rum has received much love not only from pre-Prohibition cocktail lovers but also from the ever-growing army of tiki enthusiasts.

The very dark, rich rums frequently come from former English colonies like Jamaica or Barbados (e.g., Gosling's, which is specifically called for in a Dark 'n' Stormy) and are

Speaking of drink, when it comes to barbecuing, we won't deny it: you can never go wrong with beer. But any event involving lawns, bare feet, music, and food can only be enhanced by a good summer cocktail.

Mai Tai Roa-Ae

2 OZ AGED RUM (6 CL)
1 OZ LIME JUICE (3 CL)
¾ OZ TRIPLE SEC (2.5 CL)
¼ OZ ORGEAT OR ALMOND SYRUP (4–6 DASHES)

For extra credit and/or possible snickering from your guests, serve in vintage '50s-era tiki mask porcelain cups.

molasses-based. Most of the rum consumed in the world comes from Puerto Rico—a former Spanish colony—and can either be silver, amber, or dark, with depth of flavor and body typically (but *not* always) moving in tandem with color. Pay attention to the body of the rum you are using when adjusting ratios.

There is also a kind of rum called rhum agricole, distilled in the former French colony Martinique and, under the moniker cachaça, in Brazil. Much like the genitalia of the morbidly obese, rhum agricole is hard to find but fun to play with. It (the rum, not the genitalia) is made exclusively from fresh sugarcane juice rather than molasses and is light-bodied, refined, yet unmistakably rich.

So what is the point of it all? Barbecues and tiki cocktails are actually not the answer. But they will definitely keep you from asking the question. And if that's not happiness, it's as close as any philosophers, monks, or late-night TV watchers since time immemorial have ever managed to get.

Nothing is better suited to summer's enchantments than this appealing version of the mai tai, to be enjoyed by the flickering light of wicker torches. Despite its exotic name, the mai tai is essentially a sour. Here we recommend a 2:1:1 ratio, with a two-part pour of spirit (rum, of course) paired with one part each of sweet (here, a mix of orange liqueur and almond syrup) and sour (lime).

As to the orgeat (pronounced "orh-jha"), do not be intimidated. A sweet syrup made from almonds, sugar, and rose or orange water, it is commonly used in Italian pastries and is readily available at specialty food stores. Straightforward almond syrup (sometimes sold under the name "orzata"), which is widely available and which you can even make on your own, will also do just fine. Or you can enjoy a perfectly respectable alternative without any almond flavoring at all, pouring in a full ounce of triple sec to maintain an even balance of sweet to sour.

Daiquiri

2 OZ WHITE RUM (6 CL)
¾ OZ LIME JUICE (2.5 CL)
¾ OZ SIMPLE SYRUP (2.5 CL)

Shake vigorously and serve strained or rolled in a cocktail glass.

If even tracking down a bottle of Cointreau is too much for you to handle on a lazy summer day, keep things even simpler with a classic **daiquiri.**

The daiquiri is a fair-weather classic, a blessing upon porches, beaches, and backyards of every kind. While simple to prepare, it is a hallmark of the cocktailing craft. Like its beach pal the margarita, the daiquiri should be served thoroughly chilled, so don't be afraid to shake it an extra dozen times or so. With all respect to Jimmy Buffet, we aren't huge fans of putting booze in the blender, which is messy and hard to do without ruining the drink. But you can get just as far by "rolling" your daiquiri or margarita—pouring all of the ingredients into the glass unstrained.

Variations

- For a **Brown Derby,** follow the recipe for a daiquiri, replacing the simple syrup with a teaspoon of maple syrup. A richer, more intensely flavored old-time classic that is not for every day but definitely worth trying out—let's say, when the weather isn't as fine as you would have hoped but you still feel like barbecuing. As when making honey syrup, you may want to dilute the maple syrup with a splash of hot water to ensure that it properly dilutes.

- The **Hemingway daiquiri** was purportedly made to order for the famed author during his Cuban years: 2 oz white rum, ¾ oz maraschino liqueur, ¾ oz lime juice, ¼ oz grapefruit juice.

One of the challenges of making a great daiquiri is finding quality white rum—one with some body to show off.
(This is an interesting parallel to the margarita, which similarly shines when made with good white tequila.) Weaker-
bodied rum—and unfortunately this includes some of the
most widely available brands—simply falls apart and is totally overwhelmed in a daiquiri. If you can find a white rhum
agricole, it's perfect for the job.

GETTING DEEP INTO D&D

Technology has extinguished so many cultural phenomena.
Example: the blind date. Why would you ever trust your friends
to set you up with a stranger when you can go online and do
the matchmaking yourself? The Polaroid: in its own day, this
charismatic powerhouse could make or break a party with the
images that it caught and spat out in minutes, but who would
bother wafting all those chemicals in the air when you can cap-
ture the same image on your phone and have it posted on a
social networking site for millions to see within an instant?

Much relief, then, that the culture of Dungeons and
Dragons continues to thrive well into the new century.
Looking ahead from, say, 1992, all the indicators pointed to
demise: the same would-be wizards and shifters who whiled
away their prime years in dark, 1970s-renovated basements
rolling eight-sided dice by candlelight against a backdrop of
Pink Floyd cassettes and muted Monty Python videos were
the ones who were also drawn, mothlike, to the computer
screen. Would mastering C++ and sniffing out porn on AOL
leave any time for the old fantasy role-play? Doubt pervaded
like a mist curling through the forest primeval.

We can all breathe a sigh of relief now. A saving throw

came from the advent of online gaming, which turned out to be an endless resource for role-play gaming possibilities. Now, it seems that half the world is working their way through a vicious campaign, engaged in mortal combat with a goliath—either on World of Warcraft or in some other, more purist version of the ultimate pastime of geekdom.

Best of all, gaming can be conducted without any distracting argument about which Floyd album is the best. The seedy couch and candles of the late twentieth century have been replaced with the desktop computer and the ergo-chair, so you can listen to *The Piper at the Gates of Dawn* on iTunes without any groans from the Dungeon Master. He's presiding over the game from Idaho, blasting *The Dark Side of the Moon* in a basement of his very own.

Bobby Burns

2 OZ BLENDED OR SINGLE MALT SCOTCH WHISKY
(6 CL)
¾ OZ SWEET VERMOUTH (2.5 CL)
½ OZ BÉNÉDICTINE OR DRAMBUIE (OR LESS, TO TASTE)
(1.5 CL)
LONG DASH ANGOSTURA OR PEYCHAUD'S BITTERS

Stir potion by candlelight, recite secret incantation, and strain into a cocktail glass or chalice.

Garnish with cured cherry (with Angostura) or lemon peel (with Peychaud's).

The Bobby Burns is an old, overlooked Manhattan derivative that, like a good game of role-play, can unfold in a seemingly unlimited number of ways. Single malt or blended

Scotch? Bénédictine or Drambuie? Angostura or Peychaud's? We won't presume to choose for you. Be guided instead by whatever was stocked in your parent's basement bar circa 1982, and what may well still be collecting dust there today.

The *Bobby Burns*. No one knows for sure who he was, but he even sounds like someone who may have been hanging out in your basement a few decades ago. Doesn't sound like the D&D type, though. More likely the kind of guy with a killer baseball card collection.

STRIKING UP CONVERSATION WITH STRANGERS

If drinking establishments were good for nothing else, their ability to foster spirited conversation between perfect strangers would redeem them. There is magic to a place where people of all stripes are welcome to enter and share a genuine piece of themselves with strangers. Consider the etymology of "pub": slang for public house, as in "any house open to the public." Is it going too far to say that freedom and democracy owe their existence to such places? Possibly. But if a book hasn't yet been written on the role of pubs in the ferment of the American and French revolutions, you can expect one soon.

It must also be said that drinking establishments have played a goodly role in the ferment of black eyes, vomit, illegitimate children, genital warts, loose teeth, car accidents, prostitution, personal bankruptcy, bad singing, liver disease, driver's license suspensions, divorce, urine-splattered toilets, and other thought-provoking phenomena glorified in these pages. There are advantages and drawbacks to them all. But there is a genuine affinity that is inspired by the joints where people meet to drink, and there is no downside to this— empathy is of unmitigated value.

So do us this favor: the next time you find yourself sitting next to a stranger at a bar or a pub, bring honor to the tradition that makes these places special. Don't give a thought to this person's age, their appearance, their gender, or how many drinks you would need to consume before having sex with them in the bathroom. Don't pause to consider whether this might be the kind of insane person who will talk your ear off for the next hour about the left-wing conspiracy to illegalize lawn care. Conspiracy theories are part of the charm, interwoven into the fabric of drinking culture. Recall that the Declaration of Independence is little more than a well-written conspiracy manifesto, and it was inspired under similar circumstances.

So celebrate your surroundings. Kick one back for posterity. Engage with the stranger. Listen with care to their dim-witted theories. Make sweet love in the bathroom. Drink up.

Tom Collins

2 OZ GIN *(6 CL)*
1 OZ SIMPLE SYRUP *(3 CL)*
¾ OZ LEMON JUICE *(2.5 CL)*
CLUB SODA

Shake and strain into a collins glass over fresh ice. Top up with chilled club soda.

Garnish with lemon wedge.

The Tom Collins is a chummy sort of drink that made its way from England to the United States sometime before the Civil War, when American folk were too stressed out about secession to invent their own cocktails. A member of the fizz and sour families, the collins has always been a thoroughly popular, accessible choice, and it's no wonder: sparkling lemonade and gin? What's not to like?

The original collins called for older kinds of gin that are just now starting to make a comeback: old tom (sweet, full-bodied) and Genever (closer to an unaged whiskey). So any kind of gin—from London dry to an old tom like Hayman's or a Genever like Bols—is worth trying.

INTENTIONAL BAD DRUNK

In a long life of drinking, you will from time to time start out an evening with the merriest intentions, and then, for reasons beyond anyone's control, get a touch rough. It starts, of course, with you kicking back a few too many rounds. You carry yourself away with a heated family discussion over, say, who inherited your aunt Marla's sense of humor. Then you lash out at your loved ones in a senseless barrage of foul language and bile. If you close out the night by calling your sister a slut and your oldest friend "shallow and pathetic" while urinating on your own lawn, well, some evenings just have to end that way. And it's perfectly acceptable behavior, because your intentions were all for the best.

Our moral compass informs us that being a nasty drunk is fine if it's an accident. Misbehavior, contrary to what they tell you in high school health class, isn't actually anyone's fault if it's caused by substance abuse. However:

What we do *not* condone is setting out for the evening with the express *intention* of working yourself into a hateful lather. Perhaps one of the oldest traditions in the book—in fact, it makes an appearance or two in the Good Book— drinking for battle isn't right, and you shouldn't do it. Alcohol should only be used as a crutch to spread love, good cheer, and sex juice—never hate.

The intentional bad drunk gives a bad name to booze when he or she crosses the line, and that is something we simply cannot forgive. We hope we haven't attracted the kind of reader who finds this sort of behavior deliciously appealing in any way. Because listen clearly: there is nothing, *nothing, nothing* remotely entertaining about a good, vicious, dirty drunken brawl.

That being said, if nothing will stand between you and the dark art of the Mean Drunk, may we suggest a cocktail?

Tipperary Cocktail

1½ oz Irish whiskey *(4.5 cl)*
1 oz green chartreuse *(3 cl)*
1 oz sweet vermouth *(3 cl)*

Stir and strain into a cocktail glass.

As originally set forth in the authoritative 1930 classic *The Savoy Cocktail Book* by Harry Craddock, the Tipperary was a good deal sweeter than the recipe we recommend. Any way you serve it, though, it's a powerful drink. Chartreuse is 100 proof, and then there's the Irish whiskey, which has fueled more barroom fights than any alcoholic beverage since the spiked yak milk the Huns guzzled when they weren't out on the prowl. It doesn't take too many Tipperarys to find yourself fall-down, spit-at-your-friends drunk. In Craddock's bar at the Savoy Hotel in London, if you so much as ordered the Tipperary, they would put a 250-pound tough guy from the East End right behind your chair, standing by prepared to bounce you in the unlikely event of a flare-up. The Tipperary is a mean one, but a good one. Just don't tell anyone that you heard about it from us.

OLD WORLD WHISK(E)Y

Scotch whisky is predominantly made from malted (or sprouted) barley; Irish whiskey is made from corn or barley (either malted or not). These fine specimens rarely show up in the world of cocktailing. Single malt Scotch's peaty flavors tend to dominate (though note that a blended Scotch mixes a blander grain whisky with the malted kind), and anyway neither was much available in the United States when cocktailing came into its own in the nineteenth century. All that being said, Scotch and Irish are worth trying out in mixed drinks when you feel like living dangerously. The **Rob Roy** specifically calls for Scotch and the Tipperary calls for Irish.

Particularly if you are playing with Scotch, you will want to adjust your use of other ingredients to balance out it's peaty, overbearing character. Peychaud's may work well in a Rob Roy, since it's sweeter and milder than Angostura (Angostura and Scotch: too many roosters in the henhouse), and a particularly mouthy single malt may require a heavier dose of sweet vermouth for balance.

HE'S PROBABLY NOT ANSWERING HIS PHONE BECAUSE . . .

Something happens when some guys drop into a bar for a drink. Not *all* guys, and certainly there are plenty of women like this, too. But for a certain type of person, entering a drinking establishment is a bit like the seedy version of enlightenment: the past, the future, everything outside of his immediate vicinity melts away, leaving only the dimly lit, jukebox-accompanied present. Credit card debts pay themselves off. Dinner plans are erased from memory. Jobs, promises, and obligations—basically all the heavy stuff that's piled on a guy since his late twenties—lift up about halfway through the first pint of beer and simply vanish. Bars, taverns, and pubs: experiential Botox, since time immemorial.

All this is a kind way of saying that when your significant other tells you he is going to meet a friend for "just a drink" and should be on his way to meet you in half an hour, and there's no word of him in an hour, two hours, four hours, and his phone keeps ringing unanswered, he isn't purposely trying to avoid you. He may be doing exactly what you hope he isn't doing, or he may be doing something that extends beyond your power of imagination, or he may be just sitting at the bar working through his sixth drink. Whatever he's doing, though, know this: it isn't a betrayal. You have to *exist* to be betrayed, and by the time he was waving down the bartender for a second round, you had long ceased to exist.

Zen Buddhists strive for years to enter a state of mind in which they cease to be. You got there without even trying: your significant other did all the work, sitting there at the bar, drinking you into nonexistence. Congratulations! Rather than stress about what he's capable of getting into now that you are non-being, we recommend you enjoy a cocktail at home, and enter into a nirvana all your own.

Last Word

¾ OZ DRY GIN (2.5 CL)
¾ OZ GREEN CHARTREUSE (2.5 CL)
¾ OZ MARASCHINO LIQUEUR (2.5 CL)
¾ OZ LIME JUICE (2.5 CL)

Shake vigorously and strain into a cocktail glass.

There aren't many drinks composed of equal measures of each ingredient, but the Last Word is one of them. True to form, it possesses a little bit of everything: sweet, dry, earthy, and herbaceous. If made with precision, the Last Word is way too easy to drink and, with three ingredients composed of at least 80 proof, provides a time-tested path to temporary nirvana. The Last Word is of mysterious lineage and isn't mentioned in most cocktail books, but, to all of our great fortune, was recently rescued from obscurity by the saintly cocktail revivalists who take an interest in rediscovering such relics. Meant to be enjoyed thoroughly chilled, the Last Word (like that special someone who seems to have checked out for the evening) deserves a good hard shake.

CALLING IN SICK, LISTENING TO STORYCORPS, AND CRYING ALL THOSE BITTERSWEET TEARS

Steve Inskeep, NPR *Morning Edition*:

On Fridays we bring you moments from StoryCorps. StoryCorps is the oral history project that's traveling the country, collecting the stories of everyday people.

It's a Friday morning. As you shuffle back and forth between bedroom, bathroom, and kitchen, sheets of cold rain slap against the windows. You are getting ready for work with an impressive dedication to moving as slowly as possible, reluctant to make a choice on what boring variation on the corporate casual theme to wear today. Today, you fear, the commute just might kill off what's left of your soul. In this weather, heavy traffic seems heavier, stuffy trains seem stuffier. Meanwhile the comforts of your home beckon: a relatively clean bathrobe, a fresh pot of coffee, warm radiators, and the low rambling of public radio piping out of the alarm clock. Suddenly you hear a soft guitar and Steve Inskeep's introduction to StoryCorps: *the voices of our times*. This week those intimate mobile booths have roved to . . .

DeWitt, Michigan, to hear from 93-year-old Donald Copeland and his granddaughter, Eve Bradley, about fighting terminal illness in midlife, meeting Eve's grandmother during the Great Fire of 1898, and working as a sharecropper in a West Virginia coal mine.

None of it has any bearing on your life. Are any of these people even telling the truth? But man, you could listen to this stuff all day.

In fact maybe you *should* listen to this stuff all day. As Steve Inskeep will remind you, they keep recordings stockpiled in the thousands on www.StoryCorps.org and, just in case you happen to find yourself in Washington, D.C., at the Library of Congress. If you have learned a single thing from listening to so many heartwarming StoryCorps episodes over the years, it's that you have *only this one life to live*, and it's a mighty short ride. So don't you owe it to yourself to live

today just for you? Call in sick. Stay in your cleanish bathrobe. Fix up a comfort drink, tune in to three or four hours
of StoryCorps and cry yourself silly.

Hot Apple Toddy

1 LARGE PEEL OF LEMON
2 OZ CALVADOS OR APPLE BRANDY (6 CL)
1 TEASPOON MAPLE SYRUP OR HONEY
1 DASH PEYCHAUD'S BITTERS (OPTIONAL)
3–4 OZ HOT WATER OR TEA (9–12 CL) (NEAR BOILING)
1 STICK CINNAMOM

Muddle the peel of lemon in a mug or tumbler.

Pour brandy, syrup, bitters, hot water or tea
into glass.

Stir with cinnamon stick.

Sip, and reach for a tissue.

Distilled and enjoyed in America since the seventeenth
century, apple brandy deserves an episode of StoryCorps all
its own. In the early days, it was consumed in massive quan-
tities. There wasn't much else *besides* apples to distill in the
British colonies back then. At the request of General George
Washington, one distillery, Laird & Company, helped fuel
the American Revolution by keeping the troops warm and
full-bellied on its famous apple distillate. Laird & Company
is still at it today, rendering some of the finest apple brandies
and applejacks on the market.

Some form of the hot toddy has been around forever, and
it is pretty much the only reason human civilization sur-

vived those first few millennia of pre-central-heating, pre-global-warming winters. It is very much the original comfort drink, and perfect for holing up for a day in your bathrobe with a box of tissues—with or without StoryCorps. While here we recommend apple brandy, other kinds of brandy or whisky can also be used in a hot toddy. For a worthwhile and traditional twist, try using black or ginger tea rather than hot water as a base.

HIGH SCHOOL REUNION

You know what's nice?

It's nice to get blackout, train-wreck, curb-retching, wake-up-in-where-the-fuck-am-I drunk. Not all the time. Not even frequently. Maybe less than once a year. But it is a pleasant little treat to dole out to yourself when you have earned it, when the opportunity arises—that is to say, on those rare occasions when your self-respect and composure are useless to you in any event.

If you think "self-respect and composure" are part of your birthright, you are wrong. You had none when you were in high school. And now it's time to reunite with first loves, bitter rivals, and that creepy kid in English class—the one who always wore the same Garfield shirt, day after day, and who said three words (in Klingon) the entire year, and who everyone thought would go postal, but is now a fabulously wealthy real estate mogul—and what the hell have *you* done with your life in the meantime?

That is to say, since you are on your way to your high school reunion, self-respect and composure aren't in very high supply tonight. Why bother trying to make a good impression on anyone? Why remain sober enough to engage in a meaningful conversation? You spent a sizeable chunk of your life with these people, and you can't remember having made a positive impression or engaging in a meaningful conversation with any of them—except your oldest, closest friends. And while they are here, too, you don't need to meet at a tired hotel sandwiched between an Applebee's and an adult video store to share a heart-to-heart with *them*.

As to the rest of these people? Give them something to talk about for the next ten years. Hit shamelessly on your weather-beaten high school sweetheart, whose spouse is glaring at you from across the table. Cry on your old archenemy's shoulder about the unbearable sadness of lost youth. Dance the conga with whoever gained the most weight. Make a spectacle of yourself. It's fun when there are no consequences—which, coincidentally, hasn't been the case since you were in high school.

Rusty Nail

2½ OZ BLENDED SCOTCH WHISKY (7.5 CL)
½ OZ DRAMBUIE (1.5 CL)
1 DASH ORANGE BITTERS (UNORTHODOX AND TOTALLY OPTIONAL)

Serve in an old-fashioned glass over ice, gently stirred.

Drinking Scotch at a high school reunion is tempting, but tricky. Scotch has a way of casting a warm glow on the past, smoothing out the rough edges and allowing you to connect with your surroundings. And it has a way of getting you roaring drunk, if that's what the night calls for. But Scotch, when ordered a certain way, can also work as a fairly reliable indicator of who's the pompous douche in the room. The Rusty Nail provides the perfect solution: an appealing and modest drink that won't raise any eyebrows and that balances the full-throated heft of Scotch with a unique honey-based sweetness.

No matter how basic the bar where your reunion is being held, you can always count on a bottle of Drambuie to be sitting on the shelf. Very likely the crust on its rim has been forming and thickening since you were in the ninth grade. Because of Drambuie's omnipresence, the Rusty Nail can be a standby for every time you find yourself in a bar with little going for it besides a thick layer of dust. And the great thing about this very simple drink is that there is a perfectly balanced Rusty Nail for everyone: how much Drambuie to pour should be dictated solely by your own tolerance for sweetness; the recipe given here is just a starting point. And once you find the ratio that works for you, you will have discovered a drink that, unlike your high school sweetheart, will never grow old.

VISITING THE OPPOSITE COAST

All of us who live in parts east (your authors included) and drop in to California for a few days share the same two thoughts: (1) these people are ridiculous, and (2) maybe I should join them. The issue goes a lot deeper than meaningless conversation and cosmetic surgery, which, while more common out west, are still so amply stocked in New Jersey that they pour across the tunnels and bridges of the

Hudson River into Manhattan, and then spill over into Brooklyn, across Long Island, and straight down against the Gulf Stream to Miami. Rather, for the out-of-towner grimacing through a Hollywood nightclub, or observing a mile of San Franciscans lined up for a hug from an Indian guru, the mystery we can't get out of our heads is the *complete lack of shame* on display. Everyone on the West Coast seems totally comfortable in the firm embrace of the absurd.

In contrast, the further east you call home, the more likely you are to find yourself embarrassed, all the time, about pretty much everything. Maybe it's the relative proximity to England, which invented and continues to refine the art of embarrassment (as well as the presumably unrelated craft of making gin). Or maybe it's a Darwinian phenomenon, where the obliviously sunny have always ventured westward, leaving a path of worry in their wake. Whatever the reason, Northeasterners are constantly blushing and looking askance: embarrassed by ourselves (deep down, who doesn't crave a big hug from the Indian guru?) but more frequently, as a vicarious phenomenon, by what other people are doing. Call it a saintly tendency to take the world's sins of foolishness onto our own shoulders.

The universal sense of embarrassment is rarely acknowledged outright in its Northeastern homeland. Rather, it's proudly painted up as a kind of stoicism. So as an outsider walks all tough and steady into a Hollywood nightclub, the obvious drink order—that is to say, the one that furthers her conceit of being all tough and steady—is the whisky drink.

Meanwhile, the Californian visiting New York is no doubt buoyed by the lack of vision and opportunity she sees around her. The bloated work hours and copious pounds of pale excess flesh make her more grateful for her West Coast roots.

And ordering her favorite, abusively sweetened vodka-tini reminds her that a return ticket to LAX is tucked away neatly in her oversized handbag. Soon enough she will be leaving the narrow minds and sallow complexions of the East Coast behind her. But then, in California success is always just around the corner, just out of reach—and in time this, too, grates on the soul. Perhaps our California friend is relieved to visit a place where, beyond Wall Street at least, there are few illusions about the difficulty of achieving lasting success.

It's easy to play into all of these mind games when you are out of town and sitting at the bar—easy to order something that will reconfirm your sense of self. But here is our advice to all of our readers, from sea to sea and from Corpus Christi to Detroit: the next time you are in a bar on the opposite side of the country, check your prejudices and conceits at the door. Consider yourself lucky to be out of town for the night, set down in a world apart from your own, where you might be afforded some perspective on your life. This is the opportunity to order a drink that transcends all of the definitions that you impose on yourself, and the clichés that you sometimes allow to define the world around you. Here's one for the whole damn country.

Americano

1½ oz CAMPARI (4.5 cl)
1½ oz SWEET VERMOUTH (4.5 cl)
CLUB SODA

Build in a highball glass filled with ice, and top up with club soda.

Garnish with orange slice.

Bittersweet and refreshing, this highball was invented in Milan, Italy, as a dedicated platform for Campari. First served in the late nineteenth century as the "Milano-Torino," the drink became enormously popular with American booze-tourists during Prohibition. It may seem surprising that people who were willing to travel halfway across the world just for the pleasure of enjoying a drink out in the open would be content with a choice that is not much stiffer than a glass of wine. Perhaps these booze-desperate Americans' knees had weakened, or perhaps they were just enamored of the sophistication of sipping such a delicious and quintessentially Mediterranean aperitif while seated at the street cafés of northern Italy. Campari and sweet vermouth are both Italian through and through, but Italians, perhaps bemused by the Americans' fascination, redubbed the drink the "Americano."

With a history like that, the Americano truly can be said to belong to everywhere and nowhere. Once you are accustomed to Campari's bitterness, the Americano is easy to drink and, thanks to its low alcohol content, easier to order a second or third time. With ingredients that can be found in just about any bar, the Americano is rarely out of place.

DINNER SERVED IN WHITE PAPER BOXES

Chinese takeout: the ultimate comfort food. Perhaps it's the explosion of sodium, the dense mass of noodles, or just that familiar block of dry white rice, but there is something profoundly satisfying about Chinese takeout. It's a firm way of telling the world: (1) you don't need to see anyone or go anywhere tonight, (2) you have nothing to prove as to your culinary prowess, and (3) you are not at risk of—or you laugh in the face for—high blood pressure.

As you dig into your noodles and enter the hunker-down zone of a splintered chopstick pleasure coma, you feel a nagging sensation coming from below. Nothing to be alarmed about; it isn't coming from your stomach. It's your underwear. They feel . . . swampy. Swampy like maybe you haven't changed them in three days. And then it hits you: you haven't done *anything* in three days. Your teeth are rotting off your gums. Your laundry pile is attracting flies. Even as your body begins to glow with pleasure from the buckets of monosodium glutamate that were dumped into your food, you are hit with a crisis of confidence. You are hit with the realization that when people bandy about that term "loser," they're describing—basically?—*you*.

Enter the cocktail, to restore some class and ambition to the evening. To give you a sense of purpose and perhaps even achievement. To save you from the mediocrity that has been chasing you down. If you are thinking to lecture the authors that solid cheap beer is the answer for takeout food, you may consider that we have already gotten that memo and worked through that six-pack. But only a cocktail can elevate a takeout meal into something classier, and for really a minimal amount of effort, considering that your meal has been prepared and brought to your door by someone else. Even more important, the right cocktail can stand up as well as anything to the spice and massive flavor range that frequently comes in those white paper boxes.

Aviation

2 OZ GIN (6 CL)
¾ OZ MARASCHINO LIQUEUR (2.5 CL)
¾ OZ LEMON JUICE (2.5 CL)

Shake and strain into a cocktail glass.

Garnish with lemon peel.

Let's hope your meal arrives with aviation-like speed—but if it doesn't, enjoying an Aviation is as good a way to while away the wait as it is a match for the meal. Bittersweet and, thanks to the inclusion of cherry pit in its fermenting process, strongly nutty, maraschino liqueur is very much its own thing. (If it were being unlawfully marketed toward minors, a catchier name for it might be "Cherry Almond Funk.") It is a useful cocktail ingredient—and suitable for a drink paired with almost any kind of Asian food—because it will stand up beautifully to a wide range of flavors without overwhelming them.

The Aviation was traditionally prepared with a dash of crème de violette, which gave the drink a sky-blue color—hence the name. This violet liqueur disappeared from the shelves for many years and is only now coming back. If you do find some and decide to use it in the Aviation, use a bit less maraschino.

To make up for the side dish that you ordered and paid for but was not included in your delivery—and now the restaurant isn't answering the goddamn phone, and you are really getting unreasonably upset about it, but you *really* wanted that one side dish—here's an extra recipe to cool you down:

Japanese Cocktail

2 OZ COGNAC (6 CL)
¼ OZ ORGEAT OR ALMOND SYRUP (4–6 DASHES)
2 DASHES BITTERS (ANGOSTURA OR, IF AVAILABLE, FEE'S
    OLD FASHION)
2 LEMON PEELS

Stir with ice—one peel included—and strain
into a cocktail glass.

Garnish with remaining peel.

While Japan has a worthy cocktail tradition all its own, the Japanese Cocktail is about as Japanese as that California roll that came with your order. First stirred up circa 1885 by a Yankee naval sailor, it has enough body and a hint of sweetness to stand up to whatever ethnic food you are willing to throw its way (aside from Japanese cuisine, ironically, which a Japanese Cocktail would overwhelm). Just as critically, once you get your hands on a bottle of orgeat or almond syrup, this is a simple cocktail to make. Which is ideal, given that you really are (cocktail or no cocktail) a pathetically lazy failure of a human being.

AFTER WORK

If the office is a jungle, the Irish pub around the corner is its nourishing, deadly Amazon River. There is no surer way to foster your personal ties with the monkeys you work with than sharing a casual after-work drink. Irish beer, Irish whiskey, and mediocre martinis of every color and creed are billed to the expense account, and the Thursday night good times roll. Come Friday morning, the light smiles and playful teasing continue on a quieter scale, hopping from cubicle to cubicle like exotic frogs smuggled back home in a suitcase.

Like the Amazon, though, the after-work pub is more insidiously powerful than it may first appear, and a stalking ground for every manner of low-lying reptile. Beneath the camaraderie, tensions persist, leading you to drink more aggressively than you should. Many a sturdy drinker has been pulled under by the strong current of excess in this trickiest of situations. Things best left unsaid are said too loudly; things best left undone are done with vigor (hopefully with at least an effort at concealment, in the bathroom). If the night goes the way those nights often go, those Friday morning pleasantries can mask more than a little residual shame.

That Irish pub around the corner is filled to the rafters with howlers and crocodiles, leaping and calling with reckless gossip and loose talk; watchful, predatory, and ready to pounce. And with every round, the chaos thickens, darkens, encroaches. Phantom currents pull harder. Fatality and opportunity each become breathtakingly casual possibilities.

To stay alive, we recommend frequent trips to the bathroom (alone). Check out your reflection, take stock of the situation, restore your composure. It's a long night ahead, and come morning, you'll have a job to hang on to.

Irish Aspirin

1 SHOT IRISH WHISKEY
1 SHOT ORANGE JUICE

Consume in rapid succession.

Mixed drinks have never been the Irish pub's strength. In fact, it's almost suspect when an Irish pub *does* serve anything decent other than a good pint of beer. So we recommend you play it safe as nighttime descends on the river, and stick with a Guinness. When the crowd starts ordering shots—and there *will* be shots—Irish Aspirin is a safe and tasty way to keep afloat, providing ample nutrition and hydration to prevent a call-in-sick hangover tomorrow morning. Good Irish whiskey followed by orange juice: it may not be as nutritious as that Guinness you are nursing, but it's damn near close.

Variation

If, *but only if*, you are feeling adventurous, ask the barkeep if he has any pickle juice nearby. A shot of Irish whiskey followed by a shot of pickle (rather than orange) juice is called a **pickleback.** If the barkeep gives you a hearty smile, it's because he recognizes in you a kindred spirit: the pungent, invigorating pickleback is what keeps certain New York bartenders on their feet night after night.

BOOZE AND PILLS ON THE RED-EYE

Dear reader, if you are a first-class passenger, this episode is not written for you. We offer you our congratulations. Now, enjoy your soft, pointless life of indolence and turn the page.

For the rest of you:

Life is full of indignities large and small, if you are only willing to look for them. Example: your fellow readers, the ones who just turned to the next page. You have seen these people before. They were the ones who whisked by you on a separate line at check-in. You saw them as you were prodded cattlelike onto the plane; they were already nestled into over-stuffed leather seats with legroom so excessive it could serve no purpose other than to take space away from the rest of the passenger cabin. Peering down with contempt at their trash mags, you think, *no* Wall Street Journal *for them—already made their millions, these ones have.* (Of course, the same trash mags are crumpled in your carry-on, but never mind. *You* didn't spend money on your reading material. You stole it from the dentist's office.) You shuffle by an entire row of first class dedicated to a set of four-year-old twins and their nanny. *No higher taxes for the rich,* you muse. *We mustn't choke them.*

Past the striving bourgeoisie of the business class (poor fools, tossing away their hard-earned thousands for a mere yard of seat width), you are now surrounded by the teeming squalor of economy or, as the British used to unflinchingly call it, the "lower class." Welcome home. *Wait!* you long to cry out. *There's been a terrible mistake! I'm not supposed to be here!* Much like a sullen teenager who is convinced that she was switched at birth, you are constitutionally incapable of coming to terms with the mediocrity that surrounds you at the back of the plane. The humiliation burns as if for the first time, as if you had never flown anything *but* first class. Strapped into your seat at an acute angle—ninety-degree seating apparently went the way of the meal cart—the next so-many hours of your life stretch before you as separate, quantifiable units of agony.

Fortunately, this is a redemption story.

It's a passion play: *The Passion of the Pills.*

As you contort every which way to pull your shoes off your feet, you thank the Lord for the minor injury that you suffered six months ago. More specifically, you thank the Lord for the prescription painkillers the injury earned you. Your orange-bottled savior will deliver you to your destination like a babe-in-arms and will fly in on the wings of a room-temp alcoholic beverage, served by a surly flight attendant who was recently demoted from first class for her willful lack of charm.

Madras

2 OZ VODKA *(6 CL)*
1½ OZ CRANBERRY COCKTAIL *(4.5 CL)*
1½ OZ ORANGE JUICE *(4.5 CL)*

Serve curtly, in plastic cup on ice.

Made with ingredients stocked on even the sparest of beverage carts, the Madras is well-suited for air travel. Vodka, with its relatively few congeners (the complex organic molecules that often lead to the more punishing hangovers), is a good starting point. A good three ounces of vitamin-rich, hydrating fruit juice will also help ensure that when the plane touches ground, you will awake feeling refreshed and relatively untrammeled by the effects of airline humiliation and substance withdrawal.

SITTING NEXT TO A MOVIE STAR

Your friend is twenty minutes late. *Always* twenty minutes late. Even when you try to take the twenty minutes into account and show up late yourself, your friend receives some sort of psychic signal to that effect, ups the ante, and shows up twenty minutes after that. As you sit at the bar, staring dumbly into your drink and wishing you were friends with better quality people, someone walks in and sits at the empty seat next to you (you? why you?). You feel his presence before you turn your head to make the positive ID. It is not your friend. It's _____?! *In this bar? This* is where he comes to drink?

Your eyes dart to the window for a quick paparazzi check. None. It's just you and this celebrity and whatever it is that he's radiating—and you want it. You want to be closer to it, to bathe in it, and you suddenly realize that you are every bit as pathetic as anyone you have ever judged for being star-obsessed. You won't succumb, though, will you? He probably comes here to unwind precisely because this bar draws customers who are too cool to make a fuss. Acknowledging him now would be like surrendering your cool credentials. You would never be welcome back here again. This is a test: a challenge to your self-respect and nonchalance.

But who doesn't acknowledge the person sitting next to them at a bar? It's rude. People come to bars for collegiality. In your nervousness, you gulp down the last of your drink and now find yourself sitting at a bar with an empty glass—and no excuse to be there except to violate a celebrity's privacy.

Fortunately, your next drink order, which you need to put in immediately, will provide an icebreaker. Your mother has always complimented (backhandedly) your voice as your "best asset"; here is the chance for it to be noticed. Perhaps he's just as self-conscious and unsure of what to do as you are. Maybe you should even buy a round? But then wouldn't that be strange, given the distribution of wealth and power here? Surely he would think you were hitting on him. Maybe you *should* hit on him . . . What should you order? What is he drinking? Why is he here anyway? Why isn't he acknowledging you? Why aren't you good at this? What do people who live in Los Angeles do? Maybe you should move to the West Coast . . .

Minutes pass, and your psychosis-induced paralysis continues. The window during which you can casually say hello to someone who sits next to you is rapidly closing, and your late friend's twenty-minute mark is fast approaching, and who knows how your friend will react if you haven't already set some sort of natural rapport with the celebrity? Just as you get the bartender's attention to place your order, your famous neighbor downs the rest of his drink, gets up, and leaves, taking his radiance and any hope you harbored of fame and fortune with him. *Damn.*

Mary Pickford

2 OZ WHITE RUM *(6 CL)*
1 OZ PINEAPPLE JUICE *(3 CL)*
½ OZ MARASCHINO LIQUEUR *(1.5 CL)*
1 DASH GRENADINE

Shake and serve in a cocktail glass.

A fitting accompaniment to your ruminations about *what could have been if only*, the Mary Pickford is strongly reminiscent of Hollywood's Golden Age, when naughty jaunts to Havana for the fabulously decadent resulted in a bevy of pineapple drinks, many named for the megastars of the silent film era. And Ms. Pickford was as big a star as there was; for critical claim and popular adulation, only Charlie Chaplin could claim to be her equal. While the actress's popularity faded when sound was introduced into films, the cocktail named in her honor has aged beautifully. Agricole-style rums are perfectly suited for the Mary Pickford, but any white rum of decent quality will do.

SHOPPING WHILE INTOXICATED

We all want to make the world a better place. A passion for altruism can run especially hot after a few drinks, and it seems somehow wasteful to let the public-spirited urge pass unheeded. But what can you do while intoxicated in order to be a force for good? Working in soup kitchens is a drag when you're drunk—everyone else's liquor breath starts putting negative ideas in your head. So if you really want to be of use, we recommend focusing your attentions on energizing the economy. Stimulus plans and tax cuts come and go, but *consumption* is what the modern world is built on, it's what will power the future, and it's damn entertaining after knocking back a few drinks. The half-sodden conversations and steamy dark corners that frequently accompany boozing will inevitably lead to regrettable indiscretions. But only your credit card will know the damage you have wrought when you dedicate your drinking hours to shopping rather than socializing. And it's equally engaging whether you are clicking contentedly away at your home computer or whether you are carousing recklessly down the avenue from bar to boutique.

Best of all, waking up next to that new pair of shoes is sure to bring a smile to your face—unlike waking up next to Mr. or Ms. Who-the-hell-is-this-and-why-is-she-drooling-on-my-pillowcase?

Vodka Martini

2¾ OZ VODKA *(8 CL)*
¾ OZ DRY VERMOUTH *(2.5 CL)*

Stir and strain into a cocktail glass.

Garnish with lemon twist or spear of olives.

The ultimate symbol of conspicuous consumption, the vodka martini became the "it" drink during the 1980s and '90s, and though it lacks some of the flavor sophistication that has since become more popular, it's undeniably enjoyable. Potato vodkas from Russia or Poland (our Cold War rivals who, when we were fawning for their vodka, were similarly covetous of our denim) tend to have enough body to take center stage, particularly when supported by a more-than-nominal measure of vermouth.

If you are worried about the damage you may end up doing to your credit card after nearly three ounces of vodka, or if you feel cheated because we already discussed the martini earlier in the book, here is a worthy alternative:

Black Russian

1¾ OZ VODKA (5.5 CL)
¾ OZ COFFEE LIQUEUR (2.5 CL)

Serve in an old-fashioned glass over ice.

Invented in Western Europe in the thick of the Cold War, the Black Russian must have had an intriguingly menacing ring to it when it first hit the scene. It couldn't be easier to prepare, and it's definitely tasty. If you are shopping online, the coffee flavoring will allow you to feel almost virtuous, as if you were doing real work at your computer instead of tossing away your money on the trappings of capitalism. Stalin, surely, will turn in his grave.

Variations

- For a **White Russian,** add ¾ oz of cream. Then don your bathrobe, grow a beard, and go looking for a rug.
- A **Dublin Mudslide** is made with ¾ oz of Bailey's Irish Cream rather than cream. It's an unfortunate name, but the drink is fine.

ENDLESS ARGUMENTS OVER EASILY ASCERTAINABLE FACTS

Here is a pastime that really *has* been killed by technology. Woe to the days when three or four friends could work through a case of beer arguing about the Orioles' roster in 1997. Was *Magical Mystery Tour* released as an EP or an LP in the United States in '67 or '68, and what new singles were added to the B-side? Until the turn of the twenty-first century, the only way to know for sure was to work through an entire bottle of Jim Beam and yell about it. Now some wiseass spoils the fun by whipping out his iPhone and pulling up a Wikipedia entry: late '67, LP. Even prolonged disputes carried out on turf closer to home are now extinct. Is your ex-boyfriend dating the heiress to the Tootsie Roll fortune, or isn't he? Answer, from Facebook: yes, but she looks like a real sourpuss, and possibly virginal.

We will not join the rest of the world in celebrating this information revolution. Why get to the right answer by consulting a credible authority when you can stick stubbornly to the wrong one and punch a friend in the face for good measure? Dear reader, this book is a tribute to the joy of sharing quality time with the people you care about over the perfect drink—even if that means belittling them. So for old time's sake, pretend for the moment that your flight is ready for takeoff. Power down your handheld devices, lift up your trays, and unplug your laptops. Cut off all access points to the factual record. The only way to test the strength of your friendships is to nearly ruin them by bickering as if there *is* no right answer: as if you live in a vacuum and the only path toward redemption involves repeating the same points over and over at progressively louder decibels, insulting each other's intelligence, and rejecting the possibility of your own fallibility.

Old-Fashioned

2 OZ BOURBON OR RYE WHISKEY (6 CL)
½ OZ SIMPLE SYRUP (1.5 CL)
LONG DASH ANGOSTURA BITTERS
LONG DASH ORANGE BITTERS (OPTIONAL)
LEMON PEEL
ORANGE PEEL

Stir and strain into an old-fashioned glass over fresh ice, or neat.

Twist both peels over glass.

Or is it . . .

Old-Fashioned

2 OZ BOURBON OR RYE WHISKEY (6 CL)
1 TEASPOON OR CUBE SUGAR
3–5 LONG DASHES ANGOSTURA BITTERS
1 THICK ORANGE WHEEL

Muddle sugar, bitters, and orange. Then add bourbon or rye whiskey.

Stir and pour unstrained into an old-fashioned glass over fresh ice.

Garnish with cured cherry.

Every bit as traditional as its name suggests, the old-fashioned deserves massive amounts of respect for its deep American roots and long-standing popularity. The Postal

Service owes it a stamp. It should be designated as a national park. Rich in flavor and appealingly sweet, the old-fashioned is a monument unto itself.

Equally monumental are the debates about how the old-fashioned should be prepared. The use of rye or bourbon is up for debate; rye is historically accurate but bourbon works fantastically and has become, over the years, far more common. And that's just the beginning. Muddled fruit or no garnish at all? Sugar or simple syrup? How much bitters, and what kind? Our feeling is that the answer depends partly on the depth and sweetness of the spirit you use (a sweeter bourbon will take more bitters) and largely on your own preference. But if you are looking for a debate that the authorities at Wikipedia and Google can't settle in thirty seconds, you couldn't do much better than this.

So sip, buzz, and gripe. The old-fashioned, like pointless brawls and whiskey itself, is an American tradition.

THE HANGOVER

After a nice solid bender—one that endures for, say, a long weekend, or a decade—a mild hangover can become an interesting perch from which to view the world. By day, everyone you know, including yourself, becomes distasteful to you. Not just run-of-the-mill unlikable but really thought-provokingly hateful. You develop a mutual antipathy even—and perhaps especially—toward insentient objects like door frames and bathroom fixtures, and the sun's slow path across the sky brings you as much joy as would a fingernail dragged down a chalkboard. Out of all this misery, an original worldview, the germ for a personal manifesto, Marxlike in breadth, emerges.

Liquor may be hurting your body, but your body is defi-

nitely fighting back. A low-level groan of desperation and
loathing simmers as a by-product of your system's proletarian
rebellion against the decadent, urban elite located wherever
it is in your cranium that your so-called judgment resides.
However irritably, though, you do manage to function.
Trains continue to run. The conduct of ordinary business
proceeds fitfully, and by night, with the first drink, the military junta reestablishes authority. Aches and grudges melt
away, as opiates are distributed equitably among the restless
masses. Alas, the rebellion is silenced but unquenched. In
the morning, discord finds its voice anew.

One night, the military junta uses too much force, so
to speak: you really drink far too much. As a consequence,
morning finds your temples throbbing and your inner ear
reeling. You understand, unmistakably, that this time is different. The proletarians are raging, shaking the very gates
of government. As you stagger to the bathroom for a particularly athletic, gruesome struggle with the porcelain, you
realize that today there will be no conducting of ordinary
business. Electricity, water, mass transit, the Postal Service,
everything will be brought to a standstill as the angry masses
take to the streets. It won't be pretty.

Trying to assert some order on a system that has vaulted
itself into rebellion, you dry-swallow a handful of painkillers,
but they bounce ineffectually off the barricades like rubber
bullets. Parliament dissolves in a haze of finger-pointing and
cowardice. The military junta stands by, coolly prepared for
all contingencies.

Lying flat on your back on the bathroom tile, sweating,
in deep pain, you are blessed with an improbable moment of
clarity: there will be no alcohol this evening, or tomorrow, or
the next day. This bender has gone far enough. System-wide

reforms are needed, and will be implemented, by the govern-ing elite. You will be staying in, curled up, reading a book—any book but *How to Booze*—watching a movie, cold turkey. The military junta will be disbanded until further notice. For now, your one goal is to survive until evening without sawing off your head on account of a desperate impulse to distance yourself from the pain vortex. Above all, though, the immediate crisis—*how*, exactly, are you planning to heave yourself off the bathroom floor and ensure you don't end up here again in fifteen minutes?—must be resolved. And so the military junta must be deployed, one last time.

Corpse Reviver No. 2

¾ OZ DRY GIN (2.5 CL)
¾ OZ LILLET BLANC (2.5 CL)
¾ OZ LEMON JUICE (2.5 CL)
¾ OZ TRIPLE SEC (2.5 CL)
1 DASH ABSINTHE

Shake and strain into a cocktail glass.

Garnish with lemon peel.

There are two hangover remedies that are proven to work: hydration, because your body needs it; and alcohol, because your body wants it. Various cocktails known as "Eye Open-ers" or "Revivers" served as big-time hangover cures in the cocktail heyday of the nineteenth century. The Corpse Reviver No. 2, in particular, is making a huge comeback. It's one of the oldest members of the sour family, revolutionary in its day for the use of citrus and sweet liqueur. Thanks to its balance and essentially modern approach to ingredients, the Corpse Reviver No. 2 has stood the test of time better than many other drinks of its era and purpose. It's both light and complex, and for a flavorful, really interesting drink, it goes down as easily as anything we can think of. Most important, we speak from painfully personal experience when we declare this drink worthy of its name.

READING THE GOOD BOOK

There are no standing invitations to heaven. You have to earn your way onto the VIP list, and even then your name will only be penciled in. Lightly. Any subsequent slipup and it's as if you were never favored at all. Is dedicating your life to greasing your way upstairs a wise allocation of your earthly resources? Many people think so. Others live for the moment and to hell with the consequences, which sounds romantic, but has the *carpe diem* crowd honestly considered the details of fiery punishment? Eternal damnation sounds really, really unpleasant if you bother to think about it.

If you are undecided, you need to spend some quality time with the sacred texts of Western civilization. It's time to truly consider the risks and rewards on each side of the equation. Take a week off from all earthbound obligations, and check into a Motel 6. Bring a bottle of disinfectant, and a cocktail shaker.

Left side of the bed, nightstand, second drawer down: (1) the Yellow Pages, heavily creased at "E," as in "Escort," and (2) an uncut copy of the Gideon Bible. Douse the entire drawer with disinfectant, gingerly reach out for the Lord's word, leave the Yellow Pages where they are (this is not the week for that), and set to work.

The Bible is rambling and frequently off-topic. If you approach it with cover-to-cover ambition, and you are drinking at the same time, you may not make it past the juicy bit about Lot's naughty daughters before reaching for the Yellow Pages. Better to take a more focused approach. See the following passages for moral instruction:

- Genesis 16: Childless Sarai advises her husband to sleep with the maid to ensure continuation of his bloodline. *Way to take one for the team, Sarai! Your time will come.*

- Genesis 18: The men of Sodom are so love-crazed for the three mysterious angels that they refuse Lot's offer to take his two virgin daughters instead. The daughters, appalled at Dad's offer, take their revenge by getting him drunk and bedding him down. It's worth noting that Lot isn't held responsible for incest. From this we may conclude: *Lot was drunk; not his fault.*

- Leviticus 20: This is the part with the rules—a book of manners for tribal living. If anyone mates with the livestock, it's not just the perpetrator who has to be executed. The tempting sheep must die, too. But justice is meted out delicately: for bedding your mother-in-law you will be burned at the stake, whereas sleeping with your stepmother results in an unspecified and presumably less painful form of execution. Meanwhile the married couple that fornicates during a menstrual period is punished with a light sentence of eternal exile.

- Deuteronomy 26: The hand shall be sliced off any woman who tries to defend her husband in a losing

battle by going for the groin of his opponent! Lesson?
Stand by your man, but keep it above the belt.

These are not easy rules to follow. Bestiality, dirty fighting, incest: is it worth giving it all up for a shot at eternal paradise? The New Testament has much to say about the alternatives; if the apostles are to be taken at their word, Jesus spoke about hell more than anything else.

As you weigh your options, you realize that you have lived your week at the Motel 6 like a monk in the ancient tradition: flipping through ancient texts, living off gruel, and drinking yourself into a coma. You have had a pretty good time at it, and except for the forty-five dollars you spent watching three minutes of pay-per-view adult programming, you haven't sinned once. Maybe getting into heaven isn't so hard after all. Now if only you can manage to check out of here without opening up those Yellow Pages . . .

Angel Face

1 OZ RYE WHISKEY (OR, MORE TRADITIONALLY, DRY GIN)
   (3 CL)
1 OZ CALVADOS OR APPLE BRANDY (3 CL)
1 OZ APRICOT BRANDY (3 CL)

Shake and strain into a cocktail glass.

Perhaps things would have turned out better if Eve hadn't served up the forbidden fruit. But the world of cocktails would be significantly less interesting without the contributions of apple brandy. Here is an "equal parts" cocktail with *two* fruit-based brandies. The formula renders a fruit-forward but surprisingly dry cocktail well-named and nicely balanced for accompanying a good old-fashioned Bible study. The Angel Face is traditionally made with gin, but Bible Belt rye is at least as blessed a choice.

BRANDY

Brandy is distilled from fermented fruit juice—any fruit juice. Given those wide parameters, it's hardly surprising that brandy covers a massive range in flavor and quality. For all that, most drink recipes that include brandy call specifically for either **cognac** or **apple brandy**.

Cognac is distilled from wine grown in a particular region of southwestern France. Cognac is always oak-aged for at least two years before bottling, but for cocktails we recommend V.S.O.P. (Vain and Superior Old Prick),* which is aged for at least four years. The cheaper stuff is V.S.,† the very fancy kind is X.O.

Apple brandy is a fantastic ingredient that comes up somewhat less frequently. **Calvados** is a French style of apple brandy from the Normandy region and follows quality grades similar to those for cognac. **Laird's,** an American brand, also makes a terrific apple brandy (for more, see page 90).

---

* Very Special Old Pale, actually. Though the kind of person who sips fancy cognac by the fireplace may indeed turn out to be a V.S.O.P. of the former sort.

† Very Special: but compared to what? This is the lowest designation. Possibly it was meant in that sarcastic tone that kids once used on the playground when it was still considered socially acceptable to joke about learning disabilities.

COCKTAILS WITH PEOPLE
YOU DESPISE

Life is too short to spend with the people you don't like. But life is also too short for folding laundry, anxiety, sobriety, urban sprawl, entry-level jobs, fighting parking tickets, almost everything on television, electric stovetops, flight delays, fast food, bad wine, safe sex, radio advertisements, weak coffee, skim milk, herbal remedies, private school tuition, staying indoors on perfect days, and career development. Life is too short for about 93 percent of what we do with our waking hours, but we do it all anyway. Why? Because we need to get places, earn money, avoid infection. Because we are afraid of living our lives more fully. Because we need something to regret when we are dying.

If it's regret you're looking for, regret is what you will find at pretentious cocktail parties, tedious professional events, and get-togethers with the rotten side of your family. Drinking with people you can't stand doesn't just waste time: it's a waste of calories, your liver, and good alcohol. But, like commuting and submitting to infuriating airport security procedures, it must be done.

A good way to think about drinking with the despicable is that it's preferable to the alternative of *not* drinking with them. Like almost everything in life, this is an activity that goes down easier with a cocktail. There is also a definite bright side: with your inhibitions lowered, you may find yourself saying the unsayable, and, in the process, burning bridges you've always wanted to burn. Which is great, because it means you may never find yourself wasting an evening with these people again.

Pink Gin

3 OZ MEDIUM-BODIED GIN *(9 CL)*
5 LONG DASHES ANGOSTURA BITTERS

Shake and strain into a cocktail glass.

What is it about gin? What is it about bitters? Mixed with more hospitable ingredients, each of them can be the life of the party—in fact, they may even be the two most important products on the shelf. But when gin or bitters are tried on their own, each can come across as, well—aloof. A bit difficult. Something analogous to how you are probably coming across tonight. Just ordering a glass of gin and bitters sends a message to your drinking companions, and it isn't an overly friendly one.

But don't be fooled: something exciting happens when these two charismatic but intimidating ingredients interact. The pink gin is substantially tougher than its name reveals—Angostura was used as a daily ration in the British Royal Navy to stave off malnutrition, and gin was the incentive for the crew to take it—but you will likely acquire a taste for it over time. Its subtle and very complex flavors lend themselves to sipping it slowly during an agonizing conversation—but when the time is right for an escape, it's easy to bottom-up before you cut loose from the crowd.

We recommend that you use Plymouth gin if possible. It's what the Royal Navy used—in fact they even had their own stuff made to order, with about 10 percent more alcohol content than the standard variety—and its medium body is well-suited for this cocktail.

TAWDRY HOLIDAY PARTIES

A child is born under a night sky luminous with stars, and is visited by three well-wishing kings. A tribe of Hebrews gets ornery with the local Greek imperialists. Miracles of lights and holy spirits abound.

A couple of thousand years pass, and you are drinking hard out of a plastic cup on your boss's living room couch. The human resources director has his hand on the small of your boss's back, who keeps glancing up, curiously delighted, at a piece of mistletoe stapled to her kitchen ceiling. The nervous paralegal—the one who sings lullabies when he thinks he's alone in the hallway, has a penchant for trench coats, and (it is rumored darkly at the watercooler) just last month obtained a permit to carry a concealed weapon—is stealing ornaments from the Christmas tree. The office secretary is retching in the bathroom, summoning all of her willpower to aim into the porcelain without any side splatter, while two interns agitate impatiently nearby with an eight ball one of them won in a heated game of dreidel. You are considering cooking up some mischief yourself, ideally with this certain somebody you recognize from the elevator but whom you just met for the first time right now—currently wearing a surprisingly fetching reindeer sweater and sitting right next to you on the couch.

Question: how did it come to this? Admittedly, short days and long nights can bring a person down. Drinking heavily and going wild is a perfectly reasonable remedy to seasonal affective disorder. But why do baby Jesus and Judas Maccabaeus have to be dragged into it? Why did your Secret Santa gift you a super-sized sex toy and a pack of D batteries? Strippers in red felt? Christmas-themed porn? For the love of God, *why?*

Answer: Because we want it that way. This is a post-precious world. Holiday schlock is cringe-worthy, but we can't live without the Sinatra tunes, the stop-motion animated specials, and the lit-up trees, so we embrace the traditions but can't help winking all the way through. Hence the deliciously tawdry holiday party. Hence Yuletide porn.

Holiday parties remind us of our innocence, of Santa and babies in a snowy desert pasture, and of terrific music that we can't stop replaying year after year but that the world is now too jaded to compose anew. Also, they remind us of Company Workplace Policy Memo 4, which, strictly interpreted, forbids the sexual advance you are about to make on your new friend in the reindeer sweater.

Presbyterian

2 OZ BLENDED OR STRAIGHT RYE WHISKEY (6 CL)
2 OZ CLUB SODA (6 CL)
2 OZ GINGER ALE (6 CL)

Build in a highball glass over ice.

Stir until well mixed and garnish with lemon wedge.

The Presbyterian is an understated but festive highball that can be cobbled together from the sparest of cupboards. Classic and straightforward, over the years the Presbyterian somehow got lost—strange, because it's nothing more complex than a whiskey and ginger ale, cut with club soda to dampen down the sweetness. Ginger and rye are both seasonal flavors, rendering the Presbyterian a suitable candidate for a holiday party. It isn't hard to find a home bar stocked with Seagram's whisky, ginger ale, and soda, and it goes just fine in a plastic cup. But if you are interested in classing the Presbyterian up—and this drink is up to the task—we recommend a straight rye or a quality North American blend, mixed with as fine a ginger ale as you can get your hands on. As with many a drink, the Presbyterian will hold up just fine to a dash of Angostura bitters.

TIDINGS FROM THE UNABOMBER
Doing New Year's Right

Major cities are designed to ensure that your New Year's celebrations will end in shambles. Metropolitan infrastructure can deal (barely) with everyone commuting at the same time, but it is totally overwhelmed when everyone decides to party at the same time. Too many idiots take to the streets. Too much vomit finds its way onto the backseats of taxicabs. At bars and clubs you are just a face among thousands, doomed to celebrate the big moment in anonymity while your friend fights her way back from the restroom. Private celebrations take place in overheated apartments where there aren't enough places to sit and no one knows what to do at ten minutes before the midnight hour besides flip on the TV and watch a fading pop star trying to revive his career with a three-minute performance in Times Square.

Then the ball drops. Everyone is relieved that the entire metropolis didn't just burst into flames due to an attack from Lord-Knows-Who. Then what? Turn off the TV and keep standing around in your socks with sweat pouring off your collar? As you fight for one of those vomit-splattered taxis on the curb, you vow that next year you will stay home and watch *When Harry Met Sally*—by yourself or with a loved one, it hardly matters.

It doesn't have to be this way. You *can* enjoy New Year's. But you need to get out of town to do it. You and fourteen friends and friends of friends need to get far, far away, down a dirt road, into a cabin with only three beds. No TV, or one with very poor reception. A decent music system. A fireplace and a ton of chopped wood. A guitar, if you're feeling hippy-dippyish. Ten loaves of Wonder bread and a bottle of everything, plus fifteen bottles of champagne. And a short wave radio, so you can confirm that the world isn't coming to an end before you head back to town.

Imperial Grand

1 OZ COGNAC (3 CL)
1 OZ GRAND MARNIER (3 CL)
1 OZ BLOOD-ORANGE JUICE (3 CL)
1 DASH ORANGE BITTERS
BRUT CHAMPAGNE

Shake ingredients and strain into a flute or coupe.

Top up with Brut champagne.

An original by Mr. Altier, the Imperial Grand is easy to build. On a cabin-wild night like New Year's Eve, you are best off mixing a massive tank of equal parts cognac, Grand

Marnier, and juice in the afternoon—or in the morning, or at whatever other time of day you might find yourself less than completely soused. Come party time, you will have little to do but dash some bitters into your flute, shake up your equal-parts concoction, and top up with champagne. It's a routine you should be able to manage until that winter blood-orange sun rises over the snowy backwoods horizon.

If we may say so ourselves, this is a celebratory, fairly sophisticated champagne cocktail—perfect for New Year's, in or out of town. There's nothing better than blood-orange juice for all-night partying sustenance, the bubbly speaks for itself, and the Grand Marnier's barrel-aged body provides a wonderful base for the champagne to hold onto.

THE UNWINDING

The cocktail has a higher calling. Its name is Friday night, and its purpose is to transform you from a beast of burden into a human being.

For many centuries, it was fashionable to make bone-crushingly dour pronouncements about the human condition. Example: "Man alone is born crying, lives complaining, and dies disappointe," Sir William Temple (1628–1699). Sounds like a party.

Jean-Paul Sartre was always full of jolly pep talk. "Anything, *anything* would be better than this agony of mind, this creeping pain that gnaws and fumbles and caresses one and never hurts quite enough."

No one puts that kind of statement up on their social networking site as a daily proclamation. People might gripe about being tired, or that they missed the most recent episode of their favorite reality show. But in this day and age each of us is a brand unto ourselves, and unless you are working toward a doctorate in philosophy, existential whining is poor branding strategy. It's a shame—we would gladly friend Sartre to get updates like "Hell is other people." Short and sweet; very tweetable. A welcome change from "Just back from g-doc—only a heat rash! OMG I was freaked for a minute there!"

So unless you are old, French, and glued to a café seat in Paris, your ability to call life like it is has been muted. When to channel your inner Sartre? Friday nights are no time to brood. But as the stress lifts off your back, your body exhales, and you mentally prepare for a few days of leisure, there is a moment in there—a little pause in the cycle—when you are forced to acknowledge the futility of the whole bit, work and play alike. Life's absurdity stares you down like a barbed joke.

The next moment, the storm passes and it is time to unwind. Pointless as life is, there's nothing for it but to drink, say foolish things, and engage in regrettable conduct—and that's what weekends are for. The Great Friday Night Unwinding may involve you kicking up your feet at home. Or it may entail a brutally expensive carousal on the town. However you spend those first hours of freedom, a cocktail may not be absolutely necessary, but it definitely helps.

So here is the Tootsie Pop question: how many rounds will it take to unwind you? Answer: try how many *sips*. The beauty of a Friday night cocktail is that at the moment you even begin contemplating it, you're halfway there. By the time an inch is drawn from your glass, you have already been transported and transformed. What you do after that is very much your business, your weekend, and your life.

Sazerac

2 OZ RYE WHISKEY OR COGNAC (6 CL)
½ OZ RICH SIMPLE SYRUP OR SUGAR CUBE (1.5 CL)
5 DASHES PEYCHAUD'S BITTERS
1 TEASPOON ABSINTHE
LEMON PEEL

Rinse absinthe inside of chilled a old-fashioned glass thoroughly to create an even layer, and discard excess.

In a mixing glass, muddle sugar and a few drops of water (if you aren't using simple syrup), then add remaining ingredients and ice and strain into the old-fashioned glass.

Twist lemon peel over glass and discard.

The quintessential cocktail of the Big Easy, the Sazerac is a perfect facilitator for letting go of your troubles. The way rye's spicy notes interplay with the herbal and floral qualities of the absinthe and Peychaud's is what cocktailing is all about—it's nothing less than scintillating. The Sazerac can best be understood as Louisiana's funky answer to the old-fashioned, relying on Peychaud's rather than Angostura. Invented around 1830 by local apothecary Antoine Peychaud to promote his proprietary bitters, the Sazerac has been closely associated with New Orleans's drinking culture ever since. As with the old-fashioned, every barkeep makes the Sazerac his or her own way and there is endless room for experimentation. For instance, replacing rye with cognac is a historically accurate but unconventional modification that is worth trying. This is one of the rare drinks to be served in an old-fashioned glass without any ice: that's why it's important (as it really is for any drink that's served up) that the glass be prechilled.

After a long day, the Sazerac can be deeply rewarding. And if a drink forever cherished in the Big Easy won't unwind you, no drink will.

BITTERS, PART 3

Peychaud's is an exciting product that hails from New Orleans and tends to do fabulous things for any cocktail calling for rye, Scotch, or cognac. Like Angostura, Peychaud's contains gentian root but it is considerably more floral and less intensely bitter. Its largest claim to fame is what it does to the iconic Sazerac—a cocktail that was for many years crippled by the unavailability of absinthe but is now gaining a near fanatical fan base with absinthe's return to the market. Peychaud's can usually be used instead of Angostura, but make no mistake: it will render a drastically different cocktail.

Like Angostura, Peychaud's is frequently worth experimenting with even when not called for in a recipe. Try it in a **Bitter French**—a variation of the **French 75** sometimes served at Death & Co. in New York.

THE

NUCLEAR OPTION

THE PROPOSAL

Who has the fortitude to get engaged without first taking a little booze into the system? A cocktail can very much help shove you over the edge when you need a bit of shoving, but what kind of concoction you will want very much depends on the circumstances. For this reason we owe you, at the very least, three cocktails for three different kinds of proposals.

THE PROCEDURE

When both young lovers have window-shopped for rings, discussed them exhaustively, and triangulated price ceilings, karat size, and clarity. When they have gobbled up entire weekends sniffing out wedding locations. When they have written out and then pruned guest lists with a cold, Marc Antony–like willingness to dispense with the dispensable. When they have booked that French restaurant where no one under the age of fifty ever goes to and donned their Friday night finest. When all this is in the record, it's safe to say that he knows that she knows that he knows that she knows that he's about to bend down on one knee and . . .

And it sort of begs the question: what's the point of all this again? Presumably, to formalize the relationship—a strange purpose, since you would think that the point of the *wedding* is to formalize the relationship. The purpose of the proposal, then, is to formalize a plan to formalize. And, to top it off, we are to understand this occasion to be a romantic high point of our lives?

Well, absurd as the planned proposal may be, there's no use in shitting on it now that you are knee-deep. So let's paint it up as "Celebratory Choreography." Here's what you can tell yourself when the brutally pricy bill comes at the end of the night: *you have each assumed a role in a private ritual that is a celebration of your mutual commitment.* Don't you feel better now? So when you sit down for a stuffy meal that you both know will be ending in platinum and blood diamonds, kick it off with a cocktail that's ridiculous but touching—just like the "procedure" itself.

Air Mail

1½ OZ AMBER RUM *(4.5 CL)*
¾ OZ HONEY SYRUP *(2.5 CL)*
½ OZ LEMON JUICE *(1.5 CL)*
BRUT CHAMPAGNE OR OTHER SPARKLING WHITE WINE

Shake and strain into a flute.

Top up with Brut champagne.

A pre-Prohibition sour, invented to commemorate the advent of the miracle of (guess what?) airmail. It's a head-spinning, festive champagne cocktail that's just the thing to enjoy privately with each other before spreading the news to your friends and family.

Variation

- Using simple syrup instead of honey syrup and omitting the champagne will give you a straightforward **rum sour,** a simple and delicious drink that is for whatever reason chronically overlooked by the powers that be.

"I DO NOT WANT TO BE DOING THIS"

Well, then, toughen up and just *don't.* Marriage can be great for the right people in the right circumstances, but if you're disposed to view marriage with fear, we can assure you that it's everything you're afraid of and more. Marriage is not for a lot of people, many of whom are already married. Your distinct advantage is that you *can* be unmarried—and you don't even need to hire a divorce lawyer to get there. Don't even think of trying to extend the relationship past tonight, though; it will just go from bad to worse.

It is true that the expectation to propose/accept a proposal is an acute problem in your life. But if you think that getting engaged is a viable solution then you are suffering from an even more acute failure of the imagination. So we will spell it out for you: the next six to nine months of wedding planning will be more psychically excruciating than anything you have ever experienced. And only then, once that's over and you've settled into a reluctant marriage, will you first learn what "psychic pain" even means.

Saying "no" isn't that simple, you say—but it's *always* that simple. You may be complicated, your significant other may be complicated, and your relationship may be complicated. But the solution is simple. If you dread the question that you know is coming at the end of the night—or the question you are expected to pose, as the case may be—here's a mouth-puckering, complicated drink: just what the doctor ordered for powering you up to make the difficult but inevitable choice.

Boulevardier

1½ OZ BOURBON OR RYE *(4.5 CL)*
1 OZ SWEET VERMOUTH *(3 CL)*
1 OZ CAMPARI *(3 CL)*

Stir and strain into a cocktail glass.

Garnish with lemon peel.

If a Manhattan and a Negroni shagged up, this would be the spawn. Not quite like either of its parents, though, is it? Like a Manhattan, the Boulevardier takes its sweetness from Italian vermouth and its spicy depth of flavor from rye. But the Boulevardier's Campari bitterness is much crisper and more pronounced than what you will get from the rich, almost musty Angostura found in a Manhattan. Meanwhile, the Boulevardier differs from the Negroni in two ways: first, most obviously, it uses rye rather than gin. But equally important, the Negroni is equal parts each gin, vermouth, and Campari, whereas the Boulevardier is heavier on the spirit. This makes the Boulevardier less bitter and also a bit heavier and boozier.

Musing over these kinds of comparisons may seem, to someone reading over your shoulder, like pure mental masturbation. And that's probably what it is. But making connections between drinks helps build an understanding of how mixology works on a more abstract level. This will help you remember recipes and give you the tools to invent your own. What all *that* gives you, we can't exactly say. Except to observe that better mixing skills is something to celebrate. Now that you have gained your independence, there will be plenty more time for boozing.

"HOLY SHIT!!"

To the lucky few who are genuinely, happily surprised by the night's outcome—either because you never saw it coming or you weren't sure if your beloved would say yes—let's focus on the *end* of the night rather than the beginning. After jumping up and down for a few hours, calling everyone you know, staring at the ring seven hundred times, and having sex on the couch, the sun will be rising. There's only one way to start the new day.

Bellini

2 OZ PEACH NECTAR OR JUICE *(6 CL)*
4 OZ CHILLED PROSECCO *(12 CL)*

Serve in a well-chilled flute.

A drink of celebration, fresh starts, and bright mornings is the best way to begin your period of engagement. A nice sparkling drink will also delay, for at least a few more hours, the beginning of the nightmare that will define the next six to twelve months of your life: relentless, bitter wrangling over what size Cuisinart you should list on your registry. The Bellini hails from the iconic Harry's Bar in Venice, Italy, where pureed fresh peaches were livened up with local prosecco. The kind of thick peach nectar that comes in a can—available at any Spanish bodega near you—will come closest to replicating Harry's addictive refreshment.

Side note: congratulations on your engagement. This is the last time you will be having sex on the couch.

MEETING THE IN-LAWS

It's a stiff drink indeed that will ready you for an introduction to your soon-to-be in-laws. The further along you are in the relationship, the worse the meeting will be. There's that dread of making a bad impression—Isn't this why you took yourself off the market? To stop worrying about first impressions?—and an even deeper dread of discovering that the stories about Mommy Dearest and the Old Man have been a touch sugarcoated for your benefit.

The scariest thing about scary in-laws isn't what it means for your relationship with *them*. All that neurosis you see across the table didn't just touch down from outer space for dinner only to lift back off and disappear again. It's (gasp!) an inherited trait. Carried from generation to generation. Brought like a highly resistant plague into the house. That eerie glimmer you see in Mr. "Just Call Me Dad" is, well, eerily familiar: it reminds you of someone with whom you're about to plunge into the rest of your life. As for your children? Their fates are sealed. Neurosis, the scientists tell us, flies in on a dominant gene—sure to override your perfectly perfect genes.

Ah, yes, those perfect genes of yours. Perfect—even though your parents are, actually, each profoundly insane. Which brings us around to what your fiancé will make of *them* . . . Well, perhaps we have strolled a bit too far down the dark path of your future. Perhaps it's time for a drink. After all, it's only your *life* we're talking about. No need to take it all too seriously, right? For this occasion, only the brightest, happiest cocktail will do: the liquid equivalent of whistling past the graveyard.

Fine and Dandy

2 OZ DRY GIN *(6 CL)*
¾ OZ TRIPLE SEC *(2.5 CL)*
¾ OZ LEMON JUICE *(2.5 CL)*
LONG DASH ANGOSTURA BITTERS

Shake and strain over fresh ice in an old-fashioned glass.

Garnish with lemon wedge.

The Fine and Dandy is a classic from the daisy family, meaning that it's a fancified sour—like the margarita and the sidecar, it's sweetened with orange liqueur rather than simple syrup. But unlike those drinks, it takes a dash of bitters. If you are curious why, try the drink once without the bitters; you will find the gin easily overwhelmed by the sour components, and the result is far too bright. It's an interesting lesson in what a little bitterness can do to encourage other ingredients to live up to their full potential—a good plug for the Angostura as well as those weird folks whose blood will run with yours sooner rather than later. So take heart, and give this cocktail a good solid shake. Then sit back, embrace the new family neurosis and have faith that your fiancé will be similarly tolerant of what's going on over on your twisted side of the family tree. A fine and dandy marriage it may turn out to be, but mark our words: awkward in-law encounters are just the first of what will inevitably be a long string of bittersweet surprises.

> ### Variation
> - For the **Pegu Club** (a cocktail with an equally illustrious past) use lime juice instead of lemon juice (and a bit less—say, ½ oz), feel free to add in a dash of orange bitters, and strain into a cocktail glass. Orange curaçao—we go for Grand Marnier—is frequently used instead of triple sec here. Garnish with a lime wedge.

BACHELOR PARTY

Why isn't life always like this? Oversized hotel rooms, magnificent steaks, erotic dancers, raucous laughter, and booze, booze, booze. In the morning, you are lifted gently from sleep by the sound of your oldest buddies ripping ass and stumbling to the bathroom. Your brain pounds with protest to toxins and dehydration. Your nostrils are full of the foulness of rank hangover breath and the residual sweetness of some stripper's perfume. And all you can think is: *life should be exactly like this, all the time.*

If you add up all the excellent reasons why life should definitely *not* be like this all the time, you will feel better about yourself, your family, and your future. We should probably list some of those reasons here and conclude that bachelor parties are best enjoyed on, at most, a biannual basis. But hell. Life *should* be all about strippers and steak. Enjoy the moment and try not to dwell on what the other 98 percent of the year is like. We have to think that the drink for the moment is something that you can keep flowing without fuss and that will keep the adrenaline high (as if there weren't enough adrenaline floating around the room already): something manly like . . . an apple martini. Kidding!

Red Bull and Tequila (or "Toro Rojo")

2 OZ GOLD TEQUILA (6 CL)
4 OZ RED BULL (12 CL)

Serve in a collins glass with ice.

Red Bull is one of the less fortunate trends to charge into the mixologist's workspace over the past fifteen years. It isn't exactly the most delicate of flavors, and after all it's basically liquid crack. But let there be no doubt: it has a certain value on an upbeat marathon night of hard living. In fact, now that it exists, it's indispensable. Red Bull is most commonly seen mixed with vodka, but don't be fooled. Red Bull is loaded with God knows what artificial flavors and a ton of corn syrup and it can withstand a lot more flavor than it's getting from the vodka. Have some faith in that Red Bull; it was built to withstand fire. Liquid fire. Tequila. A Red

Bull and tequila—let's christen it the "Toro Rojo"—is truly worth more than the sum of its parts. It's surprisingly balanced and both ingredients were born to bring boldness and energy into the night.

BACHELORETTE PARTY

You may have noticed that this book was written by two men. The writers frankly have no idea what happens at bachelorette parties. It's a huge mystery to all men. Occasionally, huge gaggles of young, attractively dressed women laughing deliriously are seen pouring out of a limo and into a restaurant or club. One such woman, presumably the bride-to-be, may be wearing a Styrofoam phallus on her head as a crown. This is a strange bridal ritual, and we pause to consider how it found its way to Atlantic City: by way of the Peloponnesian islands? Or was it torn from the playbook of the Young British Artists? Anthropologists and critical theorists among us, discuss.

With or without penis tiara, your goal at a bachelorette party is to let loose and explore some societal taboos without breaking any rules. And in fact the bachelorette party represents a dilemma to the prowling male: stimulating to engage with, yes, but is there any payoff at the end of the night? After countless nights of frustrating field study, we suspect not.

Enjoy your evening, young ladies. Enjoy toying with the many men who will approach your caravan—in vain— throughout the night. Play nice, be coy, frustrate them all, and party on. But you can bet your engagement ring that if your fiancé is wearing a woman's body part on his head during *his* bachelor party, it won't be made of foam.

Cosmopolitan

1½ OZ VODKA (CITRUS VODKA FOR A BRIGHTER DRINK)
  (4.5 CL)
1 OZ CRANBERRY COCKTAIL *(3 CL)*
¾ OZ TRIPLE SEC *(2.5 CL)*
¾ OZ LIME JUICE *(2.5 CL)*

Shake and strain into a cocktail glass.

Garnish with orange peel.

Though the cosmo gets little respect from the snooty corner of the mixology world, we see little to sneeze at. Pure and simple, the cosmo is a modern classic: a light, refreshing take on the basic sour. Still, as we recommend the cosmo for the bachelorette set, we hear some tsk-tsking from the corner of the room that disapproves of our stereotyping. In our defense, the hundreds—perhaps thousands—of hours that we, the authors, have spent toiling and boozing away in bars will truly amount to nothing if we are wrong in this:

Cosmos bring bachelorette parties to their full potential. *All* bachelorette parties. *Everyone* at the party will come to life. We are happy to ascribe it to an environmental influence rather than a genetic one, but there's no getting around the cosmo's uniquely feminine appeal.

If you are disgusted with our stereotyping, *fine.* We were trying to be nice. In our generosity of spirit, we won't hold it against you that a central ingredient of your favored drink is a sweetened, canned concentrate, and that vodka is about as interesting a mixing agent as Windex.

And we will even give you an alternative. Let's say we *do* have you wrong. Let's say you are a wilder type. Sexier, more (ironically) cosmopolitan in taste. Let's predict that mysterious, dark men with flattering, three-day stubble and exquisite footwear will be involved in your celebratory night, and in a meaningful way. Let's say that compared to your bachelorette party, your fiancé's get-together is just a bunch of silly overgrown boys engaged in a glorified circle jerk. Here's the drink for you:

Caipirinha

2½ OZ WHITE CACHAÇA (7.5 CL)
3–5 LIME WEDGES
2 TEASPOONS RAW (OR "TURBINADO") SUGAR

Muddle raw sugar and lime wedges—this abrades the surface of the lime peel, releasing critical oils—and add cachaça.

Shake with ice and roll: pour into an old-fashioned glass unstrained—ice, wedges, and all.

Cachaça is a Brazilian rum made in the rhum agricole style—produced directly from cane juice, rather than molasses. Only 1 percent of the cachaça produced annually ever makes its way out of Brazil; the rest is consumed with gusto by the Brazilians themselves. White cachaça is bottled without any barrel-aging and is fairly harsh stuff on its own, but it softens beautifully with ice, muddled lime, and raw sugar. The caipirinha is a terrific drink with a sophisticated, worldly appeal—well-suited for whatever kind of wildness you are prepared to embrace.

YOUR WEDDING

There is nothing more deliciously tawdry than a drunken bride. A messed-up groom: totally undignified. Such spectacles are fascinating to watch at *other* peoples' weddings, but for your own wedding, don't give in to the temptation.

- Bride tripping on her dress and twisting her ankle while hysterically laughing—*bad.*
- Rambling and/or lewd toasts from the groom—*bad.*
- Groom hitting on the bridesmaids—*bad, bad, bad!* (though sort of impressive, in its own way).
- Groom chivalrously holding his bride's veil back and trying to block the guests' line of vision while she pukes in the entryway to the kitchen—you will amuse your guests, but believe us . . . *bad!*

You should rise *above* this party, not drown in it. Let your friends and uncles drink themselves into oblivion. This should be a night to savor, to host, to be festive. That being said, one more drink can never kill you. (That is so demonstrably false, by the way: one more drink *will* kill you, eventually. But that's okay with us if it's okay with you.) If you do insist on staining the first night of the rest of your life, at least make sure to leave room for just enough consciousness so that you can consummate your marriage at three in the morning. Even a two-minute, half-conscious toss with a new spouse who is in even worse shape than you is better than nothing.

Southside

2 OZ DRY GIN **(6** CL)
¾ OZ LEMON OR LIME JUICE **(2.5** CL)
½ OZ SIMPLE SYRUP **(1.5** CL)
5–6 MINT LEAVES

Shake and strain out mint as well as ice and serve either up in a cocktail glass, or in a highball glass over fresh ice.

Lime may make sense with the cleaner, more "vodka"-style gins that have hit the market in the past few years; otherwise lemon will do perfectly.

A drunken bride is a spectacle, but a drunken bride with wine or cranberry cocktail running down her dress is just criminal. For the sake of your dignity, for the sake of your unborn children, for the sake of your photo-retouching budget, please drink something that won't leave a trace when it spills. A Southside—an appealing, zesty sour that has turned on many a vodka drinker to the charms of gin—fits the bill. As one of the few cocktails you can drink eight of while retaining the ability to walk out of the room on your own two feet, the Southside will give you the energy to keep rousing the guests onto the dance floor—and to preserve a little extra vigor for the end of the night.

BE BOOZY AND MULTIPLY

There is a thing called the Wedding-Industrial Complex. It is composed of fawning wedding planners, enterprising florists, obtrusive videographers, disgruntled DJs, the inventor of the wedding registry scanner, and everyone else who makes you feel as though you need to spend six figures for the right to marry. The Wedding-Industrial Complex is conspiring to keep a little secret from you.

Here's what they don't want you to know: marriage won't change your life much. Before the wedding, you may live together in a modest apartment or a house with some beat-up furniture and some perfectly serviceable cutlery stolen from a university meal hall a decade or so ago. After the engagement, you plan a big party. After the party, you go on a trip. Rings on your fingers and red in your bank account, you return to your modest home. It is now stuffed with products whose very existence can only be attributed to the invention of the wedding registry—brushed-chrome coffee grinders, monogrammed wine stands—that you got along fine without before and don't particularly need now. The university cutlery is unceremoniously dumped on the Salvation Army, and your evenings and weekends pass much as they did before. Same basic picture. You could go on as a carefree, childless couple, and nothing needs to change except your age, your waistline, and your sexual vigor. Any money you earn can be dedicated to travel, cosmetic surgery, and divorce litigation.

Or you can do as the Sweet Lord has commanded, and multiply.

Why do people do it? Perhaps they can't imagine just how much freedom they have to lose. Or perhaps they can't envision of how much older they will look in twenty years, once the little buggers are finally out of the house. Perhaps the absurdity and humiliation of preschool applications hasn't occurred to them. One thing is clear, though: if most people

had any *clue* what children would do to their lives, they
wouldn't dream of having them. From this vantage point, it
sure seems as though the leading cause of birth isn't sex. It's
willful blindness. It's charming in a way, except for the fact
that these children we don't need and then sacrifice our lives
for will grow up on a planet that, in all likelihood, will self-
destruct by the time they reach middle age. Which makes
the futile, selfish sacrifices of parenthood seem even more
futile and selfish than they were before.

All that being said. Having children may not be the ratio-
nal thing to do, but it is the *gratifying* thing to do: gratifying
in ways that only a parent can truly comprehend. Parenting
makes every other activity look idiotically pointless in com-
parison—but it takes being a parent to know that.

The flip side of willful blindness, then, is a dramatic leap
of faith. Leaps—especially leaps of faith, but also leaps onto
tables or into the arms of strangers—are always easier after a
cocktail or two. If tonight is the night designated for procre-
ation, you might as well enjoy yourself and refrain from looking too far into the abyss. So here's a toast to your marriage.
A toast to your ill-fated freedom, and to the monogrammed
wine stand that will one day be used as a launching pad for
sadistically dismembered action figures. A toast to the energy
you never knew you had—and that will soon be sapped out
of you. A toast to the young ones who will turn you into old
ones, and, most of all, a toast to your instinctual imperative
to spawn.

Who needs fertility drugs when our pre-Prohibition cocktail heritage has endowed us with whole-egg classics like the
golden gin fizz? By the time you are done with all the shaking necessary to get this protein party of a drink properly
foamed and chilled, your blood will be flowing. And your

vigor will increase to Stallone-like levels after consuming the golden gin fizz itself. This is a drink best enjoyed quickly, while the foam is foaming and the fizz is fizzing. There are other advantages to downing the golden gin fizz: unscientific study suggests that if you can make it to a second round before bounding for the bedroom, your procreative adventures will be as foamy and fizzy as you will need to get the job done.

Golden Gin Fizz

2 OZ GIN (6 CL)
¾ OZ LEMON JUICE (2.5 CL)
¾ OZ SIMPLE SYRUP (2.5 CL)
1 SMALL EGG (BOTH YOLK AND WHITE)
CLUB SODA

To foam, shake vigorously without ice for 15–20 seconds.

Shake again with ice for another 15–20 seconds, and strain into a chilled collins or small juice glass.

Top with a splash of soda.

MOM DRANK WITH ME . . . AND I'M FINE!

We live in an age of marginally reduced risk and sharply curtailed reward. Playgrounds are coated in rubber foam, and seesaws are a no-no. Children are forbidden from running barefoot—heightened risk of Lyme disease—but everyone has to take off their footwear just to board a plane. Disposable coffee mugs are spill-proof.

Is it wrong to bemoan the loss of fun? Some of us *liked* running barefoot and catching Lyme disease. We *liked* gashing open our skulls after toppling off seesaws and landing on rusty playground equipment. We *liked* wearing our shoes in airports and we damn near *loved* spilling scalding hot coffee all over our genitalia while driving and then suing McDonald's for $20 million in punitive damages, plus additional spousal claims for loss of consortium. Others looked at all of this and saw danger; we saw life experience worth embracing.

The zealots won. Nearly everything interesting has been spill-proofed, childproofed, or illegalized. Meanwhile, what the zealots can't regulate outright they suffocate through a heavy guilt offensive. By barraging us with half-truths and distortions, they try to make us feel too ashamed to live our lives fully. And why not? The experts have everything to gain from exaggerating the risks, and nothing to lose from stifling *other* people's fun.

For example. There are women for whom pregnancy is an exhausting, nauseating, really horrific ordeal. For some such women, a light drink at the end of the day, once they are off their feet and the nausea subsides, would make all the difference in whether they can anticipate the next day with a positive outlook or soul-draining dread. Do the media-savvy medical experts care about the plight of such women? They do not. They only care about the fact that abusive, over-the-top alcohol consumption is (obviously) not healthy for a fetus, and that the surest way to minimize overconsumption is to strictly discourage *any* consumption. Studies of moderate drinking during pregnancy have yielded results that are inconclusive at best. But why should individuals be trusted with the capacity for making nuanced judgments based on ambiguous data sets when they can instead be scared into taking the safest, dullest course of action by experts willing to distort the truth in the name of a simplified sound bite?

When it comes to moderate drinking during pregnancy, our intention is not to endorse one view over another. It's your risk and your fun, not ours. But we will point out that pregnant women have been drinking moderately for millennia and people have generally turned out fine. We will point out that staying youthful and happy ourselves is one of the best things we can do for our children. And we will offer you a great, low-alcohol drink that is sure to revitalize and relax an exhausted pregnant woman at the end of the day.

We hope you enjoy! This is an original creation.

Andalusia Aperitif

3 OZ FINO SHERRY (9 CL)
1 OZ HONEY SYRUP (3 CL)
½ OZ NAVAN (1.5 CL)
3 DISCS CUCUMBER
1 PINCH KOSHER SALT

Muddle cucumber, add remaining ingredients, and shake.

Strain into a wine glass.

Garnish with thinly cut slice of cucumber.

Light, aromatic, and at least colorably nutritious, the Andalusia Aperitif is as endearing a drink as any you might imbibe when you are expecting. And don't let the disapproving glares of others ruin your hard-earned tipple: your days are too weary and the Andalusia Aperitif is too special.

And just to make sure the point is not lost on the crowd, take the drink in a cocktail glass rather than a wine glass: there may be a more elegant vessel than a cocktail glass for delivering a fuck-you to the fear-mongering teetotalers, but we can't think of what it might be. And while you're at it, pour out some sugar on the table, give it a nice, clean chop with your credit card, and snort it all up. Then pat your belly salaciously, hissing out in a loud whisper for all to hear:

Just a taste, my precious little bunny. Just a taste of what's to come.

NAVAN

Navan is a natural vanilla bean liqueur made by Grand Marnier. A neutral grain is flavored with macerated vanilla beans for several weeks and then combined with cognac.

DRINKING AT THE PARK

What are you *doing* here? It's 8:45 on a Sunday morning. You should be in bed, passed out, slowly rousing yourself into a brutal hangover and a quiet morning of self-loathing and coffee. Yet here you are with the other chump dads, lamely watching your young ones tear through the park. While your wife sleeps, deservedly, after an endless night of nursing and midnight tantrums, you squint into the sunlight with the words "What have I done?" furrowed into your brow. You're doing the right thing, but somehow you never thought it would come to this. And let's face it, it never should have.

You thought your life would turn out differently. It might comfort you, or maybe it might not, to learn that *everybody* thought their lives would turn out differently. Exceptions are crushingly rare to demographic truth. You are a yuppie, and this is what yuppies do. Throughout life, there are dark moments of weakness, humiliation, and shame—many of them are described in this book—and they call, desperately, for something called *liquid dignity*. This is a concept we have no doubt inherited from Hemingway, and though we didn't want to get you down by mentioning it too early in the book, we should note that the need for liquid dignity is a primary reason for boozing. And boy—do you need it now. So rinse out that flask your boozy old granddaddy gave you on graduation day; it's about to come in handy. Just make sure you stay alert enough to intervene on the jungle gym—a concussion will be hard to explain to your wife, particularly with whiskey breath.

Mint Julep

2 OZ BOURBON OR RYE (6 CL)
¼ OZ SIMPLE SYRUP (4–6 DASHES)
5–6 MINT LEAVES, LIGHTLY CLAPPED BETWEEN THE
    HANDS OR PRESSED ON A HARD SURFACE

Stir and strain over fresh ice.

Garnish with 6–10 fresh mint leaves, blossoming out of the glass.

Flasks thirst for bourbon. They were made for each other, just like parks were made for children and drunken fathers.

The mint julep may have gained its fame as the tipple of tony horse races and languid summer days, but as a playground refreshment it's beyond reproach. Sugar content should be quite low—note this drink calls for a third as much simple syrup as we typically recommend—and if possible use plenty of shaved ice. When serving the drink at home, in the extremely unlikely event you happen to have a julep cup in your cupboard (it's typically pewter or stainless steel, slightly wider at the mouth than the base), you probably know that's what you should use here. Otherwise use an old-fashioned glass or something slightly taller. Garnishing the julep with an abundant bunch of fresh mint leaves is central to this drink; your nose should be buried in the mint leaves when you sip so that the overall experience is largely olfactory.

All of these fussy guidelines aside, the mint julep is palatable and even oddly appropriate when strained and funneled into a flask, ass-pocketed, and lukewarm.

Variation

Cognac mint julep: like many classic American whiskey drinks, the mint julep was likely first served with cognac.

SURVIVING SLEEPOVERS

Little pissants.

Charming enough when you see them at a pizza party here and there. But when they invade your home, stake out the basement with obnoxious music, and whine through your precious evening with a thousand little complaints and food peculiarities, you suddenly realize that other peoples' children are far less lovable than your own. And this epiphany may lead to another: maybe your own kids are unlikable, too?

You may also wonder how you will survive the night without stuffing the lot of them into the minivan and dumping them off at a deserted gas station on the highway. We recommend a more sensible course of action:

1. Put them to work chipping ice.
2. Make yourself and your spouse a few pitchers of booze.
3. Set the sturdiest kid to work with the shaker.
4. Sit them down in front of some relatively harmless porn, effectively shutting the lot of them up for the next nine hours.

The feedback from their parents, while perhaps not as severe as if you abandoned the lot of them at a highway rest stop, may not be entirely positive. But your night will be salvaged, and the kids will have learned a few things about mixology and the merits of manual labor instead of wasting away the evening screeching at insipid horror flicks on your widescreen television. Pissants.

Odd McIntyre

¾ OZ COGNAC *(2.5 CL)*
¾ OZ LILLET BLANC *(2.5 CL)*
¾ OZ TRIPLE SEC *(2.5 CL)*
¾ OZ LEMON JUICE *(2.5 CL)*

Shake and strain into a cocktail glass.

An original by Harry Craddock in *The Savoy Cocktail Book*, the Odd McIntyre is rarely served but definitely appealing. It's a refreshing drink—like the related Corpse Reviver No. 2, part of the extended sour family—and because the spirits' work is evenly split between brandy and Lillet Blanc, it's reasonably light on the system. As an equal-parts cocktail, the Odd McIntyre is so easy to mix that you might even put one of the kids to work with the measuring cup.

REALIZING YOUR CHILD IS A FUCKING IDIOT

All we can really do in this world is try our hardest, watch in horror as our efforts come to naught, and hope it turns out better for the next generation. *They won't make the same stupid mistakes that we did*, we muse—and the young ones are quick to agree on this point. The problem arises when you, as a parent, realize that one or more of your children are completely incompetent. Then you realize that they aren't even capable of functioning at a high enough level to make the kinds of mistakes you made, and they are too clueless to know what's about to hit them.

If you look back to your own youth and can recall a specific time when your parents started to drink more heavily, you might experience an epiphany: your parents hit the bottle precisely when they realized *you* were a fucking idiot, too. So it's no wonder you feel drawn to the booze shelf more and more frequently right about now, as your dumb-ass eldest ambles into the kitchen and stares at the open refrigerator for a good ten minutes before wandering back to the computer like a zombie.

Greyhound

2 OZ VODKA (6 CL)
GRAPEFRUIT JUICE

Pour vodka in a highball glass over ice. Top up
with grapefruit juice and stir well.

For those of us who find orange juice's sweetness a bit
too cloying, the greyhound provides a refreshing and distinc-
tive alternative to the **screwdriver**. Grapefruit juice shows
up only rarely in cocktail recipes—it wasn't widely available
during the formative years of the mixed drink—but it's a
well-balanced, usefully puckering ingredient. Needless to
say, the greyhound is simply prepared and open for enjoy-
ment at whatever time of day you happen to witness something particularly deplorable from your half-wit child. And
the greyhound is packed with all of the good, healthy stuff
that will keep you living long enough to support your children through their mid-forties.

Variation

- For a **Salty Dog,** sometimes served with gin rather
  than vodka, salt the rim.
- As even your idiot prince can tell you, a **screwdriver**
  is made with vodka and orange juice.

Stage 4

Eulogies,
Etc.

MUMBO'S LAST RIDE TO THE VET

One painful element of losing your household pet is that no one else cares. Sure, family and friends may lend you a sympathetic sigh—before steering the conversation back to an update on their newfound passion for book clubs. To work colleagues, a lost pet makes about the same impression as a missed train. But the reality for someone who loses a pet is that it's *really sad*. On a scale of mourning, it won't rate as highly as losing an old friend, but it's embarrassingly close.

Even other pet owners don't particularly care. For twelve years you pass the lady with the frizzy hair in the street walking her dog while you walk yours. Your entire relationship is premised on a common passion for braving the outdoors in the middle of a downpour for the privilege of picking up canine fecal matter with a plastic bag for a glove. Then one day she sees you shuffling down the street, no dog, no plastic bag, a total mess, tears in your eyes. She hears the news: *Mumbo's passed. We had to put him down.* Oh, she pushes some half-hearted sympathy your way, meanwhile thinking, *Mumbo? That's what that dog's name was? Never knew* . . . Frizzy Hair says the nice things, the right things, before passing along. There is no mistaking, however, her lack of genuine interest.

And why should anyone feel compassion for you? Caring for a pet is profoundly self-indulgent, an unjustifiable allocation of resources in a world where most of the population is starving. If you want to spend a few grand a year for the right to vacuum dog hair three times a week, people will look past it. That money could also support an entire orphanage in sub-Saharan Africa for a year, but who's counting? Just don't expect much sympathy when the jig is up.

For pet owners, the moral fuzziness and emotional strangeness of loving a pet makes the pain of loss no less real. And the very, very worst part about it is the final ride to the vet:

The affectionate hug. The sad canine eyes. The familiar panting (slowed and pained, it's true) from the backseat. In the waiting room, forlorn patience from dog and master: what else is there to do? You limp into the back room and play a part in the unthinkable. Then the lonely drive home. No panting from the backseat, just eerie silence. For now, all of the callous nonsympathizers with their moral high ground and theories of transference can go screw themselves. This hurts.

Improved Cocktail

2 OZ SPIRIT OF YOUR CHOICE (6 CL)
3 DASHES RICH SIMPLE SYRUP
2 DASHES ANGOSTURA BITTERS
2 DASHES MARASCHINO OR ORANGE LIQUEUR
1 DASH ABSINTHE
2 LEMON PEELS

Stir all ingredients except for one lemon peel and strain into a cocktail glass.

Garnish with remaining lemon peel.

To understand what makes the Improved cocktail an improvement, consider for a moment the old-fashioned—a member of the oldest family of mixed drinks known collectively as "bittered slings"—made up of nothing more than booze, sugar, water, and bitters. The bittered sling is a winning combination to be sure, but rudimentary. The Improved earned its name as an upgrade, made possible with the introduction into the United States of a host of exotic ingredients like fancy liqueurs (e.g., orange or maraschino liqueur) and absinthe. And while we like our cocktails the old way as well as the new, "improved" is by no means an unfair description of what a little flavored liqueur and absinthe can do to a drink. Europeans would never think to water and mix these precious ingredients, but to gas-guzzling Americans, "waste" is a relative concept: hence American dominance in cocktailing and NASCAR both. With its use of fancy liqueur as a sweetener, the Improved can best be understood as a template for all the drinks invented at the cusp of the twentieth century that will forever reign ascendant; it is here that the margarita, the Manhattan, and the sidecar must pay their respects. If the old-fashioned is a Neanderthal (and never a more charming Neanderthal there was), the Improved is a Cro-Magnon.

What does any of this have to do with losing Mumbo? Very little, since we don't care about your stupid dead animal. But given the flexibility inherent in the Improved—any kind of gin or brandy will do particularly well—it's nice to know you can make this at home, using whatever you have handy, without having to show your gloomy face around town.

LAID OFF

On the day you receive the bad news about your job—i.e., that you no longer have one—the facile advice you once gave to your laid-off friends will come back to haunt you. All those rousing halftime sermons you gave about this being the opportunity of a lifetime suddenly ring hollow. When you enjoyed the comforts of a steady paycheck and a dependable, if dependably stifling, routine, visions of a more inspiring future danced in your little head. But your morale is suffering from the unexpectedly cold snap of rejection that accompanied the pink slip. Your coffers are running low. The next stage of your life wasn't supposed to kick off like this; it was supposed to happen on *your* terms. A future as an entrepreneur/singer-songwriter/country innkeeper strikes you as a bit less compelling right about now. To your own dismay, you find yourself working every lead you can think of to weasel your way into a new job as similar as possible to your old one—in other words, right back into the same life you were leading. The same life that wasn't all that fulfilling anyway.

It is now *our* turn to step up to the podium for a rousing sermon. Here we go:

Herodotus, the Greek historian, recounted how the Persians made decisions. He reported that it was the Persians':

> general practice to deliberate upon affairs of weight when they are drunk; and then on the morrow, when they are sober, the decision to which they came the night before is put before them by the master of the house in which it was made; and if it is then approved of, they act on it; if not, they set it aside. Sometimes, however, they are sober at their first deliberation, but in this case

they always reconsider the matter under the influence of wine. —*Histories of Herodotus*, 1:133 (trans. Davis, 1912)

We like this. It's a fairly accurate description of how we wrote this book. And we think it's a damn fine way to claw your way out of pink-slip depression and into a life of your own choosing. Any future worth holding onto will require a bit of inspiration and bravery—stuff you may not feel while sitting on the floor in the Career Planning aisle in your local library. So act like an ancient Persian. Turn to the bottle for heroic vision, and then let your sober midday self cut back the excess and determine what's feasible.

Your future is there for the taking . . . a cocktail just may be the price of admission.

Herb Saint

1½ OZ GIN *(4.5 CL)*
1 OZ ST-GERMAIN ELDERFLOWER LIQUEUR *(3 CL)*
½ OZ LIME JUICE *(1.5 CL)*
2 SPRIGS FRESH DILL
7–8 LEAVES CILANTRO
TONIC WATER

Gently but firmly press the herbs on a flat surface or in the mixing tin, then pour remaining ingredients.

Shake and strain into a highball glass—in fact *double* strain, using a mesh strainer or a tea strainer if you have one. Top with tonic water.

Garnish with lime wedge and sprig of cilantro or dill (optional).

The Herb Saint is another of Mr. Altier's original creations. It admittedly requires a bit of artistry, but what else can you do with all that time on your hands? Masturbating, social networking, and self-laceration will only take up so much of your day.

This is an aromatic, floral, and we think exciting variation on the gin and tonic: extremely palatable, morning, midday, and night. Fresh herbs and elderflower liqueur are—there's no other way to put it—*life-affirming*. More life-affirming, might we suggest, than your recently departed career. So if you truly are ready to swear off the corporate world that has recently shoved you out, then stay positive, strive for a fresh perspective, and be a hero: get off the grid, plant your own garden, and start harvesting herbs aplenty for a daily dose of the Herb Saint. You will never look back.

LAST DRINK BEFORE AA

Throughout this book we have been careful to skirt the uncomfortable if glaringly obvious fact of your craven addiction to alcohol. Don't be embarrassed, now. Alcoholism happens to the best of us. It isn't the end of the world. From our perspective, the stained breath, the suspended licenses, the pickled liver, and the mounting sick days are regrettable, but somehow necessary to a greater cause. In a certain light, it's all quite romantic. The irritating, really charmless thing about becoming an alcoholic is that everyone wants you to stop drinking. Now, you can drive your loved ones away and keep chugging merrily along: always a fine option. But you can't very well (1) admit you have a problem and (2) set out to fix it without, in fact, cutting out booze. Like, forever. And that sounds just awful.

BITTERS, PART 4

In July 2009, Modern Spirits (the environmentally responsible producer of the all-organic Tru vodka and Tru2 gin) held a bitters competition to celebrate the lost craft of bitters-making. Mr. Altier's own Baked Big Apple bitters, featuring Hudson Valley green apples, cinnamon, and gingerroot, was one of three winning selections (it won first prize in the "fruit" category) that will be distributed by Modern Spirits starting in 2010 as the first certified, all-organic bitters collection in the world.

If you are on your way to an addiction support group, we strongly recommend you say good-bye to alcohol with a drink: one final, sweet, and perfectly crafted cocktail to toast the countless good times you've had. We are confident, totally sure, that you will stop after that one last drink. One drink will be just enough. Then you will lock up the liquor cabinet, throw away the key, and mosey along to the meeting. It's going to happen *just* like that.

Hudson Monarch

1 OZ RYE WHISKEY (3 CL)
1 OZ APRICOT BRANDY (3 CL)
2 DASHES BAKED BIG APPLE BITTERS
BRUT CHAMPAGNE

Shake, strain into a champagne flute, and top up with Brut champagne.

The Hudson Monarch, another of Mr. Altier's own inventions, is fruity but amply structured. We recommend it here because you shouldn't have to say good-bye to booze without the help of a little rye, a little brandy, and a little champagne to send you off into sobriety's cold tundra. Enjoy the meeting— sounds like it will be a blast.

Two hours later, as you hack away at the liquor cabinet door with a fire ax, consider whether the next time you have your "last" cocktail, you might try something less whimsical than the Hudson Monarch, to, like, bring more finality to the situation.

So for your *last* last drink, try this:

Arsenic and Old Lace

1½ oz GIN (4.5 cl)
½ oz ABSINTHE (1.5 cl)
¼ oz DRY VERMOUTH (4–6 DASHES)
½ oz CRÈME DE VIOLETTE (1.5 cl)
1 DASH ORANGE BITTERS (OPTIONAL)

Stir and strain into a cocktail glass.

Garnish with lemon peel.

Crème de violette is hard to find, and perhaps now is not the wisest time to bring a new bottle into the house. But Arsenic and Old Lace is an extraordinarily good cocktail, and who can really think of swearing off booze without a good-bye kiss from gin? Given its strong pour of absinthe, this enhanced martini will leave an impression—while its flavors are delicate and floral, its effect on the system is anything but.

> ### Variation
> • Insist on continuing the farce by refusing to purchase a new bottle of crème de violette? Don't fret: you can still make the classic (and classy) **Tuxedo No. 1** without it. Cut the absinthe down to ¼ oz and keep the other ingredients as they are. Orange bitters strongly recommended.

For the next dozen or so "last" drinks, try this: unscrew a bottle of Irish whiskey, tip your head back, and chug. Who needs all that ice-stirring, lemon-peeling, and bitters-dashing, anyway? Cocktails always were just a bunch of bullshit.

TOASTING THE END OF DAYS

It's not as if we didn't have any notice. The warnings have been piling up fast and furious for a few millennia. And when the end finally arrives—dark red sky, cities aflame, twenty-four-hour news coverage mercifully silenced—the smell of vindication won't just be emanating from the crazy guy on the corner waving a placard. It will be coming from you, your neighbors, and, however hypocritically, all those bastards who made fortunes bringing on doomsday by over-leveraging pension funds, strip-mining coal, and subdividing farmland. Everyone who has a finger to point and a rearview mirror with which to make historical predictions will feel a sense of smug satisfaction, even as they scramble to grab what's theirs and ammo up for the inevitable man-eat-man aftermath. Saints and heroes are few and far between. Hence the chaos and destruction before you. And really, did we ever do anything to deserve something *other* than hell on earth?

So be grateful the young ones arrived at the party before the music stopped. Be grateful that there will be no more "breaking news" coverage about topics that are neither breaking nor news. And just take it all in stride as best you can. All things told, the end of days marks a fine time for a cocktail, so gather up the last of your melting ice and settle onto the porch for the ultimate showdown. Just remember to load up the AK-47 in case someone tries to mess with you before your drink is finished.

Spiced Colada

2 OZ SPICED RUM (6 CL)
2 OZ COCONUT CREAM (6 CL)
1 OZ LIME JUICE (3 CL)
1 OZ SIMPLE SYRUP (3 CL)
½ OZ LEMON JUICE (1.5 CL)
½ OZ PINEAPPLE JUICE (1.5 CL)
1 DASH ANGOSTURA BITTERS

Shake vigorously or, if the electricity is still running (this is one drink for which we do recommend a blender), blend with 4–6 ounces of crushed ice. About half a cup of fresh pineapple can be used instead of juice if you are using a blender.

Strain over fresh crushed ice in a highball glass or tiki cup.

Garnish with a generous dash of Angostura bitters over the top of the ice. Umbrella, pineapple, and cherry are each optional garnishes.

Because there is no better way to bear witness to Armageddon than with shameless frivolity, put yourself to work on prepping the ultimate in laid-back drinks. The spiced colada is a variation of the classic borrowed from one of our favorite watering holes for tropical drinks, the Rusty Knot in New York.

> ### *Variation*
> The traditional version of the **piña colada** (which is the official drink of Puerto Rico, we feel compelled to mention) can be made with 2 oz of rum, 1.5 oz of coconut cream, and 3–6 oz of pineapple juice.

However you go about mixing your drink while the world goes up in flames, do try to use Coco López coconut cream if possible. If you don't have any in your cupboard, try raiding your neighbor's house. And grab whatever else you can find while you're at it. No need to obey the rule of law now.

YOUR FINAL DRINK

Our lives are slipping past us, and few, if any, can boast that they will leave no fruit to wither on the vine. There will come a time in each of our lives when no opportunities are left to fritter away. Nothing left, seemingly, but a final chance to make peace with choices that have already been made. A last few moments to ponder: What the hell did I do in an office for forty-five years? Why is there a tattoo that says "RACCOON" on my ass cheeks? And why didn't I kiss Lisa Schiller at the seventh-grade dance?

Deathbeds aren't any fun. What's really a downer—besides the horrendous pain, the aforementioned regret, etc.—is the irritating fact that all the people moping in and out of the room will carry on with their lives well after your lights go out. And in fact your death will just serve as one minor event among many that will mark their lives. No matter how long or well you have lived, that part just won't seem fair.

At this late hour, you seize on a new conviction: everyone should go at the same time, and be done with it. And as it happens, that time should be *right now*. You suddenly gain some respect for those pharaohs with their buried wives and servants, and you start feeling out your children, your grandchildren, and the nurse staff to see if anyone is willing to go along with the new plan. Just as you start calling out for a giant vat of poisoned Kool-Aid, someone ups the morphine dose and the room blurs. All you feel is that fuzzy remorse again. Lisa Schiller! Damn her!

All we can suggest to quiet your fixation on Lisa Schiller is that minimizing the possibility for deathbed remorse involves an act of willful blindness. Training yourself, over time, not to look back at all is the surest technique for ensuring there will be no final, futile moment of regret. If that's too much to chew on, and if no one in the room seems game for live burial in the family pyramid, then the next best thing we can offer is that you spend your last few earthbound moments stirring up a good drink, settling into your favorite chair, and enjoying one last indulgence—with no pause for introspection at all.

Does your heart ever stir to the spare, solemn call of funereal bagpipes? Then the Rob Roy, a Scotch-based variation on the Manhattan, is for you. This well-loved classic is evocative of Scotland's rough, rural majesty but also, like the Manhattan itself, unmistakably urbane. It is as worthy a drink as any to sign off with.

Rob Roy

2 OZ SCOTCH WHISKY *(6 CL)*
1 OZ SWEET VERMOUTH *(3 CL)*
1 DASH ANGOSTURA OR PEYCHAUD'S BITTERS

Stir and strain into a cocktail glass.

Garnish with lemon rind or (more traditionally) maraschino cherry.

How you prepare the Rob Roy has everything to do with your choice of Scotch. A complex, peaty single malt may stand up to a generous pour of vermouth and may not require any bitters at all; a Highland single malt or any smooth blend might call for less vermouth and go beautifully with Peychaud's. And no Scotch, no matter how top-shelf, should be considered off-limits: the drink will showcase the spirit's strengths beautifully, and in any event, what are you saving the stuff for now? Just like your insistent regrets, your useless bladder, and the pain-in-the-ass dentures that you have been cursing for the last decade, your beloved home bar isn't coming with you. Sad to say it, but this time, you are leaving the booze behind.

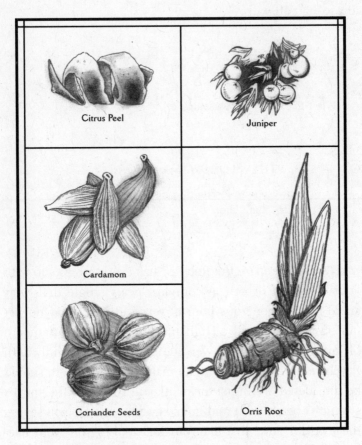

Common botaincals used in the production of gin.

STOCKING UP

The Drink Index (page 181) should help you quickly find the recipes you would like to make by ingredient. As you will have noticed by now, some drinks call for more obscure ingredients; other, equally delicious drinks can be made with sugar, lemon, ice, and a bottle of booze. So we have tried to organize recipes in the index accordingly. The drinks at the top of each list can be made from a fairly spare cupboard; the drinks at the bottom can only be made by someone with something bordering on an unhealthy obsession with cocktails. And there are a lot of drinks that fall somewhere in the happy middle.

SPARE CUPBOARD

A very basic but serviceable bar should include bottles of dry gin, white rum, white tequila, cognac, bourbon, possibly Scotch, and of course vodka if you like it. Some specific reminders on choice of spirit:

- There are fantastic, versatile dry London-style gins like **Beefeater** that don't cost much and do terrifically in most recipes.
- Bottles of white rum and white tequila should both be of good quality. Unfortunately, the cheapest and most widely available brands are not likely to have enough body to hold up in the most common drinks like margaritas and daiquiris.
- A V.S.O.P. cognac. No need to go for the priciest X.O. stuff, but a cheaper quality brandy will drag down a drink.
- Bourbon is another spirit that you don't necessarily have to spend a lot of money on to do great things for a cocktail. **Maker's Mark,** for instance, renders a terrific old-fashioned or Manhattan.

You should also have at least one kind of orange liqueur, preferably either **Cointreau** (a triple sec) or **Grand Marnier** (a curaçao) and, if possible, both. Small cans or bottles of club soda, tonic water, and ginger beer are a good idea. You will need bottles of sweet and dry vermouth (though remember, they won't last long after opening, so buy small) and last but not least **Angostura bitters.**

And you know what? While orange bitters aren't usually thought of as indispensable, once you have a bottle you will never go without. **Regans' Orange Bitters No. 6** is difficult to find in a store but can be easily purchased online.

WELL-STOCKED

A well-stocked bar should include absinthe, a good bottle of rye (**Sazerac** is a fine, inexpensive option), decent Irish and

Scotch blends, **Campari**, maraschino liqueur, green chartreuse, **Peychaud's bitters** (available online and at very useful
stores), and **Drambuie**, if you like it. Apple brandy may also
be a good idea. And if you like juice- and soda-based drinks,
you should have small bottles of ginger ale, cranberry cocktail, tomato juice, and whatever else excites you. A wider selection of rums, tequilas, and gins can also start to enter the
picture.

GEEKED OUT

From here, the sky is really the limit and it just depends on
which recipes appeal to you. It's high time you invested in a
medium-bodied gin like **Plymouth**, a good amber rum, and
some **Bénédictine**. Apple and apricot brandies are, at this
point, essential. Some orgeat or orzata syrup will allow you
to explore the dangerous world of tiki. Look online to find
the more obscure ingredients—in most places you can order
and have them delivered to your doorstep very easily.

Speaking of geeking out online, if you are interested in
exploring the vast store of recipes that *aren't* included in this
book, www.cocktaildb.com is an outstanding resource, put
together by some of the leaders in the field. David Wondrich's
drink tool at Esquire.com is also fun and easy to use.

REFERENCES

We are deeply indebted to the research and skill of leaders in the field, past and present: Dale DeGroff, Gary Regan, Robert Hess, David Wondrich, Ted Haigh, Julie Reiner, the legendary Harry Craddock, Crosby Gaige, Jerry Thomas, and the Beverage and Alcohol Resource (B.A.R.). Many thanks are also due to the hardworking and talented folks who toil away in the New York bars where much of our research and learning took place: Milk & Honey, Death & Co., PTD, Pegu Club, Clover Club, and the Rusty Knot, to name a few. If our half-assed attempt at explaining the science of booze was insufficient to satisfy your curiosity, we recommend the following resources for more credible information:

The Joy of Mixology: The Consummate Guide to the Bartender's Craft, Gary Regan (Clarkson Potter, 2003)

The Essential Cocktail: The Art of Mixing Perfect Drinks, Dale DeGroff (Clarkson Potter, 2008)

Imbibe!, David Wondrich (Perigee Trade, 2007)

Vintage Spirits and Forgotten Cocktails: From the Alamagoozlum to the Zombie 100, Rediscovered Recipes and the Stories Behind Them, Ted Haigh (Quarry Books, 2009)

The Savoy Cocktail Book, Harry Craddock (1930; Pavilion reprint, 2007)

The Essential Bartender's Guide, Robert Hess (Mud Puddle Books, Inc., 2008)

Jerry Thomas' Bartender's Guide, Ross Bolton (1887; CreateSpace reprint, 2008)

ACKNOWLEDGMENTS

Both authors would like to thank all of their friends and family members; Stephanie Meyers and Jessica Regel, for their invaluable contributions and support; Jocelyn Kaye, for her love and support, and for tolerating the authors' endless nights of "research"; Jonathan Stokes, for digging this idea up from the archives; and the memory of Jack Tripper.

DRINK INDEX

BRANDY DRINKS
(COGNAC, UNLESS OTHERWISE NOTED)

SPARE CUPBOARD

WELL-STOCKED

GIN DRINKS

SPARE CUPBOARD

WELL-STOCKED

GEEKED OUT

RUM DRINKS

SPARE CUPBOARD

WELL-STOCKED

GEEKED OUT

TEQUILA DRINKS

SPARE CUPBOARD

GEEKED OUT

VODKA DRINKS

SPARE CUPBOARD

WHISKEY DRINKS

MISCELLANEOUS USEFUL LISTS

ABSINTHE

CAMPARI

CHAMPAGNE